Walking with the Vain Cattle

*In the Womb of Life, the Plant of Miracle
Is Ready to Blossom a White Flower.*

Amal A. Islim

BALBOA.
PRESS

A DIVISION OF HAY HOUSE

Balboa Press books may be ordered through booksellers or by contacting:

Balboa Press
A Division of Hay House
1663 Liberty Drive
Bloomington, IN 47403
www.balboapress.com
1-(877) 407-4847

Because of the dynamic nature of the Internet, any web addresses or links contained in this book may have changed since publication and may no longer be valid. The views expressed in this work are solely those of the author and do not necessarily reflect the views of the publisher, and the publisher hereby disclaims any responsibility for them.

The author of this book does not dispense medical advice or prescribe the use of any technique as a form of treatment for physical, emotional, or medical problems without the advice of a physician, either directly or indirectly. The intent of the author is only to offer information of a general nature to help you in your quest for emotional and spiritual well-being. In the event you use any of the information in this book for yourself, which is your constitutional right, the author and the publisher assume no responsibility for your actions.

Any people depicted in stock imagery provided by Thinkstock are models, and such images are being used for illustrative purposes only.
Certain stock imagery © Thinkstock.

Photo cover picture: Taken by Amal A. Islim
Cover design: Fernando Sancho

Printed in the United States of America

Library of Congress Control Number: 2011905589

ISBN: 978-1-4525-3395-7 (sc)
ISBN: 978-1-4525-3397-1 (dj)
ISBN: 978-1-4525-3396-4 (e)

Balboa Press rev. date: 5/11/2011

WWTVC

Those mystic impressions

Volume 1 :

"Cultivating my nature"

A self-development book

Inspired by:

The divine order

An original spiritual drama

Soon to become a theatrical musical

Titled: *"Leeloo is hiding behind me!"*

Index

This book is about different periods of my life that may help you define a phase of yours.

It can be read from any chapter and then in order. Enjoy the meaning behind the lines, and see how it connects with your own life, inner questions and being. You can use this book as a guide of observations, realizations and for spiritual growth. Enjoy the ride.

About the author

Amal A. Islim is a Jordanian who left her homeland at the age of 17. She has travelled the world ever since, and has lived in Germany, England, Canada and the United States. She is a psychologist and life coach who has lived for the past 14 years in Switzerland. Islim writes when her soul calls for expression and finds inspiration in her faith in an ideal world.

Synopsis

ꝏꝏꝋꝋ is a sensational journey that speaks of the pains of the

spiritual growth process along with its miracles and magic.

The exploration of the inner world,

The fight of the ego versus the spirit,

Materialism versus spiritualism,

Personal ethics over blind conformity,

While still having to face the evils of this world,

yet maintaining reason and balance.

Amal Salim declares war upon her closest companion, her ego, which

she names '*Leeloo*' in **ꝏꝏꝋꝋ**.

As she begins to contest her dominant ego, she starts to feel out of

balance and suffers from identity crisis; finally she becomes aware that

she has deeply suppressed the mighty in her idealism in order to succeed

in the materialistic system.

Amal walks through her life as if constantly walking the plank; feeling lonesome around most; facing her heart breaks, and suffering cold truths one after the other; knowing that she is different, as if she was water on fire, therefore, refers to herself on occasions as *fiery waters* in *wwtvc*.

She realizes that she suffers from chronic social un-satisfaction, repulsion to mediocrity and mendacity, and profound disappointment in the greatest part of human kind, but fortunately, keeps her hope that one day she'll be united with the rare great ones.

Her discontent is predicated on the fact that most people are so far from the potential perfection created within them, and beyond that, there is more petty, and ill spirited exchange than good. This has caused her deep grief, extreme isolation, suffocating annoyance, and boredom; wishing that human consciousness expand to its sublimation along with her own, and discovers a new way to fight evil other than with evil itself.

Thank heavens, she finds true refuge in her artistic creations, while still trying to find her *"Conjunctio"* her perfect union with herself and the divine, the only place where time ceases to exist, and she feels protected, all is truthful, harmonious, serene, whole and well.

At this point of *Amal's* life, she stops being able to earn her living "as a psychologist/ senior consultant for multinationals and departments heads"; burdened with the sorrows she carries, accompanied by an unjustified cultural and social guilt, fearing to be once again among and one of the world's corporate killers; therefore, unconscious self-destruction spread its wings as if she was calling upon the mystical Phoenix, which he appears as one of the silent characters of this book, while she is consuming herself in the fires to rise again.

She orchestrates her own failure, wreaks all kind of havoc in her life by accumulating bills, leaving her job, forcing the ones who love her to desert her, living off unemployment insurance, denying herself any kind of security.

She now refuses to live a comfortable life entombed with suppressed frustration together with absent passion and flame, the void of meaning, conscious, and noble aim.

Amal starts to listen to her witness-self through daily prayers and meditations; she begins to wrestle with her own satirical vision, and acceptance of the ways she interprets herself and the universe, aware that she must seek, find and if not weave a new, and a higher form of life.

While deep transformational forces are in the works, *Amal* feels her soul migrating from living outwards inwards to inwards outwards, from her darkness to her light, navigating through her new insights on solid grounds to exhume her inner treasures buried in the depth of her soul.

In her philosophical autobiography **ⴍⴍℭⴔℭ**, *Amal* longs for a world where forgiveness is not perceived as weakness, wishing for like-mindedness, genuine uninterested kindness in herself and others, and finally everlasting peace.

She imagines enjoying a beautiful emotional life filled with joyous creatures, divine creations, love, happiness, light and justice.

But alas, she knows that evil's putrid spirit is among us and festers in our fears, also always ready to devour on our wars, ignorance, vanity, greed, and pains; wondering, "If love is the answer, why does the question still reign?!"

She rips herself away from her past life, and what she has hitherto acquired, then leaves on a soul's journey, armed with nothing but with her inner strength, supreme faith and awareness of her absolute need for growth, self-change, self-conquest and the presence of answers.

With but 20 SF in her pocket, *Amal* parachutes into a new life, naked of her ego, facing the uncomfortable but exhilarating adventure, and embarks on a two years spiritual journey, facing her inner struggle, and challenging her pride by acknowledging that she must learn compassion, and master the tolerance of what she defines as an intolerable.

Not knowing where to go, live or whom to meet, but knowing that her heart and angels will guide her, believing that *"When a man* is willing and eager, God joins in..." Aeschylus, Great Greek dramatist.

After the first publication of her book **ᘯᘯᘜᐯᘔ** in 2009, *Amal* met sponsors that are now financing her theatrical musical *"Leeloo is hiding behind me"* which is based on this book/ her spiritual journey.

Also soon, she will be working among some of the best artists, singers, performers of our times.

ᘯᘯᘜᐯᘔ is written in subtle abstract poetry, prose, philosophy, prayers, music, songs, dialogues and slam. *A unique art style that she named "AI88".*

Amal declares "The plant of miracle blossoms in its season for those who set their mind free, and dare to follow the call of their hearts no matter how insane it sounds, and against all odds. Finally she states: "The supreme faith does pay."

Meaning, that believing in your divine path helps heaven to support you.

But first, let's **walk** with her from the beginning of *Walking with the Vain Cattle,* and so the story goes...

Dr. Leona P. Heart

Review

Walking with the Vain Cattle is an astonishing journey that is based on contradictions and oppositions. It is unique, genuine, spirited, filled with anguish, deeply disturbing yet entertaining and illuminating.

Its authenticity lies in its driven-ness, particularly the distress and agony that speak from it. Amal Islim decides to go beyond herself to reach her wholeness, and understand her boundaries between her heaven and her mundane.

The tone of a spiritual drama reflects its concerns. It is auto-ironic, visionary, confessional, esoteric, triumphant, endearingly witty, obsessed with introspection, and ultimately empyrean in its aspirations.

Walking with the Vain Cattle is a journey that takes the traveler from states of extreme duress to moments of ecstatic bliss. And while ever and again it seems as if the journey itself were the goal, it appears equally obvious at many times that the ultimate goal is nothing less than the mystical union with the absolute.

Prof. Jacques Blancochemi

Review

Walking with the Vain Cattle is a unique spiritual drama in its way of thinking and writing. It is expressed through poetry, prose, philosophy, prayers, music, songs, dialogues and slam that are confessional and painfully truthful.

This remarkable author of our time speaks of her fight with the ego versus the spirit, personal ethics over blind conformity, while still having to face the evils of this world and maintain our centre, reason and balance.

Walking with the Vain Cattle takes you on a journey from the darkness to the light with images only your soul can capture. It is the author's personal journal of her materialistic fall and spiritual redemption. A duel between herself and all the intriguing characters whom she meets upon her Odyssey of chasing freedom and happiness to reach everlasting harmony.

Maitre William Salvador

Dedication

Dedicated to light workers, ascendant masters, world and earth angels in all times, who carried me through when I thought I was alone, as well as to all those on their way to the journey of light.

I also would like to dedicate this book to

the loving memory of my friend

Samer W. Bakri with this song / poem titled "Heavenly laughter".

I can still hear your laughter in my wake,

And can still feel us move and dance.

You put my heart at stake,

From the first glance.

Those golden eyes, hearts, they did break

Lovers didn't stand a chance.

You were a divine friend, and a true brother,

Not like any other, so kind,

Yet, gracefully you pranced.

How I grieved you, you know that!

I wept till the constant trance.

I thought my sorrow would never die,

And why advance?

The ache now is waving goodbye,

As I dreamt of you in Zion enhanced.

For all the joy you gave to the world,

With an open heart without a why,

Escorted by a jubilant light,

Shied even the south of France.

When with you, my world was complete,

In any land.

We crossed bridges, traditions and seas,

Trust in hand.

Live today as if there is no tomorrow, we used to say.

Come to us life, come what may!

We played, laughed, shared, and loved,

Yet the sudden arrow of death was lanced.

Oh romantics, how we suffer!

We need the perfect, and the forever.

God loves you so took you young,

Where the first best song was sung;

Then gifted you the ultimate key,

But can you still laugh and see?!

Who will call my name now and make it home?!

Lonely without you my destiny is.

Who will praise with me a storm?!

And see life as an amusing quiz!

Who will lose themselves with me and roam?

And around a fire drink a thing with a fizz.

But worry not, my friend,

This is sadness not my end.

My heart with faith will someday mend.

As the soul of the rose in its perfume is,

In its radiance and glow.

And the soul of a man in his love is,

Because in his eyes it shows;

And God in heavens with his angels is,

Some things we just know.

And you are now a celestial star, and it is so.

Keep a place for me by your side,

O, will you?

As I believe in a paradise where you reside;

And by their rules you still don't abide.

When my time has truly come,

Will you meet me at God's gate?

We still have a heaven's ride,

With angels again we'll celebrate.

And if life will beat me to become old, and gray,

Smiling wisely, yet raddled, and frayed,

Know that I am waiting for the day

To live by you, within the heavenly laughter,

Your heavenly way.

"He who knows others is wise. He who knows himself is enlightened."

—Taoism: Lao-Tzu

27th of January 2007

What's that stillness?!

What's that sound?

Is it silence?!

That drives me to numbness,

With no ground?

What's that game?!

Is it my mind?

Going insane?

What's that question?!

Who am I?!

That old refrain—

In vain, in vain.

—From the present work: Chapter 9: Stillness sound

Chapter 1

The Wish

Upon the secrets of the Caribbean Sea,

Under the most ancient tree,

I stood tall, in subdued melancholy,

Feeling that the arms of the world are not large enough,

Either to hold me or retain my grief.

I gazed at the evasive shimmer of the fair red moon,

As I listened to its hesitant echo in the luminous black waters,

Embraced by that mystic presence;

I knew it was time. Time to wish:

For happiness to come reaching and caring

And for my eyes to encompass and dare its marvellous sight,

Still, my emotions have the immensity to endure its supreme, pure blessings.

But, alas, my banished heart,

Surfing every wave that was destined to crash upon the rocks.

O, Goddess Aphrodite, with your legendary smile of joy!

Will you show me that world you're smiling at?

What is that thing you know that has eluded me?!

What is that magnificence you see and I can't?!

Will you teach me how to compose, sing, and roam the tango dance?

Will your light pierce my horrific dungeons haunted by shadow play?

Just to get me through this infinite day!

Will you at least give me a reason

To endure my war against my freedom of strife—

That incessant quest for peace, profound delight, and adoration.

I arose alone from the clapping crowd

Celebrating New Year's Eve of 2003

Leaving that long table filled with empty dishes and tasteless inspiration.

At that moment, I had to witness a larger world,

More sublime than their faces and mendacity.

I addressed myself straight to the sky,

Beseeching rescue from a world I couldn't face—

Epitomizing mostly repulsion and disgrace—

Hoping that a star would pay attention

To this inner alleged adult that is screeching in my pretended ear,

His recurring questions:

Where are you?! Who are you?! What are you doing?! And why?!

That mirrored stranger that does not cease to bewilder me!

A wanderer who is always longing for another peak experience

And constantly willing to pay the inflicted consequences from its comfort,

Just to let loose that free dreamer that has so much faith in the ideal universe.

I'm searching for that nostalgic moment of brilliant exultation,

That high sensation, that enlivening rush

Pushing myself further to another voracious edge,

Without safety, without a net

To measure my vital limits as I grow and learn to live,

To a place unreachable by a human pass,

But, maybe, by his centre and soul.

But sadly, prisoner of my own limitations,

A lesson I reject to be taught—too strenuous, too consuming!

Damn it, I'm too mortal to transcend space and time,

But as long as I survive, I promise myself

I will not relinquish trying to penetrate its realm;

Even if the price is my verve and bereavement.

To justify my anguished long-lived survival,

I had to ask the numinous for numerous changes:

First, for my soul purpose to reveal its face,

Next, joy, my heart to recognize, know, and feel!

Then the un-purged emptiness and ungodliness anchored within me will

dissipate.

And ultimately, that glowing happiness will fill my being with love and light.

But peace, I reckon that the wish master cannot be hurried.

Chapter 2

But Peace!

I reckon that the wish master cannot be hurried,

In new suffocating patience, I lament my woe.

I remained apart, as I normally am and do,

From a profoundly disturbing earthly world,

Yet neither in reality am I in, nor out of it.

Not belonging to any scheme or affection.

Foot in and foot out, my order in my disorder,

That mysterious chaos that gives me balance and guards me.

That so-called madness that keeps me sane,

As people live their routine, so my soul, I equally will train.

I returned to the music, and festivity,

Wearing that mask, its grin that aches its face,

Which ruptures progressively the child

That is hidden behind those grimaces,

Leading me further to the nowhere,

Only to dance perfunctorily under a fictitious rainbow,

That flickers as an iridescent studio rain.

Hold my breath, hold my wish,

Engraving it on my individual core—

Meanwhile, still movement, vague transportation . . .

Chapter 3

The Journey Towards
the Higher Self

3rd of November 2007

Annexe 1: Fly!

Still movement, motionless transportation

To the terminus—illumination.

Is there a speedway to a paradise?!

Can I teleport? Or simply fly?

If I throw well my dice!

Who will be sane enough to lie with me on a blanket's mist

And in this matter give me some advice

On instantly penetrating the sky,

Leaving this earth without a tie!

But then I'll miss the journey's scene,

By being hopelessly so keen!

Getting there without the adventure is less ecstatic,

However, surly, less painful and less traffic.

Is it comfort that we choose?

Out of fear to win or lose?

Is it climax that we seek?

Without the Olympic effort!

Sitting on our sharp-edged chairs,

Pretending it's not our treacly blood we leak!

I want those impediments and victories,

Before I give my last valedictory.

I love my hazards, and uncertainties,

I don't call for a forged sovereignty.

I know that's not in fashion,

But life without risk is as love without passion;

Tasteless and stale, revolting and pale.

Yet my Utopian fascination trusts in the fairy tale.

So I put all I have on the line

Hoping life will gift me the ultimate line,

The greatest break, where nothing is left to fake.

Patience, I advise myself, till my dream be reified,

Any treat after the bitter is much sweeter and amplified.

As the taste of a green apple after hunger,

Or that semidetached hug after sad solitude,

That placates me, yet in lassitude.

While struggling, I numb the hour;

Buying myself happiness by being patient, and enfolding the sour.

I know I shall take my time and become serene,

But in between—

Existence, will you just show me what you mean?!

Oh time—quick time, foe time—

I wonder if I can charge you with crime!

For turning my white shirts into red,

Yet not allowing me at my age to kindly reign.

Why are you so disloyal, and cruel?!

Why are you so scarce to recharge my fuel, and my every dime?

I believe my divine soul still hasn't found its real rhyme!

Meanwhile, I transmute in still movement, and motionless transportation

Yes, I searched myself, but as a fool.

But now, I shall wait, I shall take my time.

Every time I make a shortcut it cuts long

And I find myself further from my chosen road,

Lost in the middle of choice, frustrated, and yet bored.

Is there a code to crack for the happiness bank—

Often! Sometimes.

Sharp we are to have, and swift to cordially thank.

A quick fix but against natural physics,

As in a love liaison, when we bind them faster to our hearts,

Quicker they repel, run the other way,

To draw another curve on another chart.

Annexe 2: Take the train!

To be "reasonable", take a train,

But no train I know is prepared for such a long, rough ride—

The journey towards the self to the self,

Which is essential to my soul's main.

Where to start?! Bring me back that edifying chart.

Maybe by healing my past wounds, and sighs!

Forgiving my scars, and freeing them from their bars.

Knowing my mind as a saint knows his gods,

Then growing, to spread the elixir blithe—

To myself, then for all; what are the odds?!

But first, I must control what controls me,

No more to my ego will I nod.

I shall re-organise my meaning

And reevaluate my path,

Realign with the divine, and redo my math.

For that must I hunt, or cast a rod?

Then, I shall venerate myself as I revere the heavenly.

Isn't this gifted devotion worth a few tries?!

The heartrending price is so many bemused goodbyes.

Visibly, who fights need some space.

But in anachronism—that's my frequent place.

Why am I so out-of-the-way?!

Why am I persistently in my savage grace?

Why do I keep sliding out of track?!

Why is everything in my face?!

Why is this tunnel so long?!

What is that dreamy bloody pace?!

Why does heaven's breath stay out of my trace?

Care to join me in my erratic quest? I shall ask you not.

Don't say: "Fascinating, I'll meet you, but . . . "!

No answers in my dungeons for you I know!

This auspicious journey can't be shared,

Not to censor, or to cut.

I still have my deserted roads to pave, and light,

And when they are smooth, they will soothe.

My friendless nights will soar to breathless heights.

I must start by facing my inner fiery companions,

Those who reside in the so many me.

And shadows too, won't free me, or let me be.

Maybe next stop, nature will call, and take control.

I'll be bidden to sit under an antediluvian banyan tree

And let her fruit branches twinkle wisdom upon my mystification.

In the sparkle of an eye,

The milky crop will murmur to me the secret code,

Before, I count to three.

For now, in this life force's shade, I shall hide.

Too many questions, I shall investigate.

Meanwhile, my source I will nourish, and irrigate;

Till I know of that which abides.

Annexe 3: Just walk . . .

Step one: Every mile at a time!

Fine! Maybe I should walk every mile at a time—

Perchance, I'll find my true reflection—

Till I smile in gratitude for what I've evolved into,

For those long steps with a natural extension.

Those footprints I've marked on my shores,

Prevailing over every peril, and every roar.

I can cross the muddy paths,

I might wade in confusion and anguish,

But head high, strutting with no help from finery.

Undeniably "in" the legendary feast for heroes

I will be, and we'll unite,

With my heavenly supporters giving me the proud ovation,

Without the must for Gucci or Dior.

On my way, must leave the vain, and the bore.

Those who don't aim high,

Searching their souls is not their goal.

They just keep moving to survive the day,

Without investigating any divine door.

So they live, so they die—aggravated with qualms,

Importuning fate, "Why can't I possess more?!"

My courage is in my backpack—

For my odyssey, which I will decipher then track—

Along with that rose knife I found,

Not so sharp, but it will do

To kill a surprising monster

Without a hassle or a sound.

Or cut a forest's trap,

Or frighten an inferior hellhound

That attacks on any front.

I'm trying to keep out of danger in my every hunt,

I'll fight if I must, but I'd much rather not.

I avoid distractions to attain my light.

But careful, I just might—

Might noxiously bite.

Step two: Facing the monsters

Faced by those endemic others,

Those who dread your difference, and indifference.

If you don't howl with them,

You better have much resistance.

So wisdom, advise me please!

Nice idea the walk, one step at a time,

But halt! Let us reexamine the compass,

To console my volcanic rumpus.

Shall I accept the party's mask?

To blind my enemies from my sight!

Do I make them think I'm one of them?

To bring them comfort and perhaps delight!

Do I fake their joys?!

Eat their food?!

Howl their bark?!

To get along or to get by!

And when we play the game for so long,

Don't we become the game?!

And winning the match has lost its reasons,

Whether for tomorrow, or tonight!

What a dilemma! Dilemma indeed!

Step three: Do we fall to better see from beneath?

So reason, will you give me whatever advice?

As insight I surely lack, not vice!

Shall I walk grandly yet withered from dignity?

Shall I keep my head high among swinging blades?

Shall I my humiliation conceal whilst being stoned at?

Shall I simper whilst swaggering on my knees?

Or is it spontaneous for a soul's soldier

To march on his stomach with simulated ease?

It's ignorant to ask for the evident, I know.

But not another frugal burden, not another price!

I must pay for the redemption!

For virtue, I never favoured.

Chastity—I enjoyed its concept.

How simply flavoured!

But now, I choose the righteous stand.

From hell, I must be banned.

I had to do my mistakes,

I had to put my life at stake.

I had to learn what I don't know!

Now, in debt to life, that's all I have to show!

I have been in the wrong!

I thought then it was my dance and song.

Now, I'm in shame,

For chasing the ephemeral affluence, and the dignified fame

So my guardians, enough, please!

Will you stretch me your hand?!

Maybe exile me to a safe haven in a safe land!

Now I will purify my soul, and plead my case.

Stare at myself till I see my face.

Then harness my growing path, quite discreetly.

Find my inner wealth, rather completely.

In time, announce my hidden light,

Then shine to shame the rumours of evil—

That there's not enough hope in this world,

No need to dream, no need to chase.

But if I stand my ground,

And crisscross with an angelic face among thugs,

Will they let me survive those bugs?!

Smashing against the shield of my drive,

Blinding my sight, to clasp their coarse bounds!

Those professed heroes!

Why not kill superman to become the man?

Splendid thought, not as bad as it sounds.

A plain distraction to help you forget,

That you're not the hero,

But merely trading your soul as a courtesan!

Who cares about the tact of the dance!

Take the chance and assassinate me

On the charge that comforts you.

A paragon of virtue! No! That will comfort me.

But why not for a moral truthful stance!

I'm raising the ethical flag in a brigand's world!

Surely, "pas à la mode" and not the jive!

But I'm not superman, not even a man.

And that is my perfection.

But does that limit my questions, sorrows, and tensions?

I'm fraught as you are, and yearn not to be the idol,

But to achieve a soul that's free from struggle and bridle.

What shall I do while in between?!

Shall I wear the lion's face in a virtuous, peaceful soul?

Shall I hide my goodness, and decency's trace?

But then, if the supreme is hidden,

Where do I find it beyond myself?

How do I decipher the gentle from the evil?

By intuition?! Great idea! Revolutionary pace!

But sometimes, when in chaos and in need,

With a defeated inner pride, and waning moral strength,

Don't we doze off that inner guide into stupor?

To allow the acceptance of the alarming scene!

Isn't there the world's dwelling—

Precarious to the outsider, and clamorous "still" to the insider?

Those faithless growing demands that feed on our urgent needs,

Speculating the next best deed!

Where is the promised heaven?!

The unswerving super! Or shall I go back to sleep...!

Where the dream is arousing, yet cheap!

Step four: Wipe my face clean

The only rescue is when all alone,

When we can take off the second face, the accepted one.

Relax, and be merry, then watch the comedy show

Where everyone is partly good!

And everyone is "Hollywood-how" eventually happy.

What a relief, this spectator sport!

In this rest of semi-guiltless coma,

I conceal myself within the armour of a facade-enchanted world.

Oh, phone rings . . .!

The second face is back in place.

But again, whom are we entertaining?

Must the show really go on?

Are we soothing them or ourselves?

What a fooling case!

What a worthless, stagnant race!

In the midst of the night, I hold my breath tight.

I try to sleep, but I want to weep.

No tears in my soul; frustration is what I reap.

I close my eyes wishing for a dream, where things may seem,

As if heaven removes the curtain, and reveals its magnificent scheme.

But again, the wish-master can't be rushed.

Until he salutes me I take time to wonder—

Will I handle now the seventh heaven's great heights?

Or will it just give me the vertigo?

Rising amidst angels naked without wings,

Wondering if roaming among their globes is just a fling!

I still need to comprehend the cause of my fight.

I'll take my time; in my speed to light, I'll try not to rush!

Step five: Strutting to the Guillotine!

Leeloo! Ego! Or spirit, today!

I am bearing the vicious, smoky forests, searching for that sign

That beacons its presence to the light address.

This inert, persecuting, boundless marathon—Where is its end?!

But another truism I run into, a new choice, one more test.

The Lotus Elise! Stand still! Or, kill the evil pest!

And when it's all over after I've chosen well,

Will I be parcelled up with red ribbons, with a noble wreath upon my head?!

Finally, the badge before I'm dead!

Or, maybe, swathed in celestial dew in the morning's trust!

While Cupid rejoices my just momentum and thrust!

For manifesting the beauty's love of the divine— ultimately that panacea!

Where I feel my heart ache with awe and gratitude

For being part of the whole, and one with all

When I connect with my abundance source,

Where all is well and "light-speed" from hell!

Riding away on my unicorn, or any bloody horse!

When a miracle finds its home, and resides in my heart.

Or shall I merely settle for sangria with a tortilla!

It's another kind of fill!

But I reckon life is not enduringly "à la carte."

Swell plan—desires tolerance, honour, and skill.

Very well, to the highest bidder, I will not promote my soul.

But, why not go for the comfort and the ball?

No, not I! Whatever my consequences must be,

My dignity remains above all.

Heavens will back my divine call,

While contemplating an innovative, common constitution,

Deciphering ever after happiness on a guiding hill.

Or do I just sit here as an unsettled bill?

Surrounded by barking dogs that I didn't order,

In a quiet frenzy, wishing to cross that common border.

Quite possibly, I am just clinging to another hallucination.

Another mirage of hope, to survive those doubtful moments,

As awaiting a pure black iris to miraculously plough up through the

desolate grounds.

Or hungering to share love in the house of serpents and hate,

Where respect, confidence, and admiration are just theatrical bait,

Depending only, on today's market rate.

In this barbaric panorama,

I scrutinize numbly the roots of my own deracination.

Oh, Guillotino! Be sharp, be swift.

Get finally my drift! Or not quite still!

Step six: Who is the victim?

I had to understand the weak, those victims of the slaughterer,

As I was the slaughterer, in another space and time.

I was a warrior. I fought for what I believed was just,

For the glory of that reason, the cause of which I don't remember anymore.

And every time my blade approached my sheep's necks,

It was certainly not to shave or groom them.

But does that pretext my need for the meat?

I must leave the sheep in the city of Willows,

Now knowing that someday my lord I must meet.

I'll leave them in His presence, in peace.

Also, maybe, build them a wood's hedge from that tree I butchered,

To protect them from the heinous;

The outfitter fox is rarely me anymore, but, sometimes, it would be thee.

Isn't it the rule, when we care for something, we should set it free?

Running wild, in hoaxing paradoxes, we are trained to endure to be.

Step seven: Rise above my contradictions!

Under the ambiguous star of contradictions and multitudes,

I was born. A holy choice!

The symbolic sign of Christ! That Capricorn!

Which voice?

His upper goat strives for the earthly skies,

Yet his lower dolphin yearns for the depth of heavenly seas,

Where is that balance and choice's ease?!

Call it fate, and lie stretched in between?

On the surface tormented yet risk clean!

Or, shall I rationally plunge into the unseen?!

Killing a part of the self is quite mean.

But a choice imposes; a choice to capture the dream.

Step eight: Walking with the Vain Cattle

We also tolerate to bear those vain spirits who await the eternal life,

Promised to them by the lord of vanity of hell.

That's what he can afford as a name.

He would refer to himself as a deity, but sadly he perishes like you and I.

So he asks his devious queen to command,

As he's allowed the freedom of only one step at a time.

Oh, that chessboard is even limiting for a king!

Order your majesty, when you must wear that royal ring.

She appears to promise an illusionary never-draining power,

An ally, in her everlasting inferno

The fee! Reverence by the weak—

The weak is any applicant searching to recuperate his lost respect, and pride.

Qualifications: No morals please!

"Vain amateurs welcome," the advert invites,

As long as for you the goal justifies the means.

"Need a guide?! No trouble at all! Follow the hand, follow the lead!"

She incites, "Carry the pirate's flag, and bellow with me an earth-shaking growl:

'Aaouuu-Aaouuu! We are the soldiers of war."

So you succumb to the search, thinking, "I've met my captain!

Who will lead me to my glory; question being: hers or yours?

But that's a dangerous question to ask at this point, just trail the commander,

Be content that your clever master can vanquish the enemy.

Problem being, you could become the enemy,

And with a spirit like that you eventually will be,

The moment you will give up the slave's name tag.

Easy boy, don't be hasty! You are a second rate slave.

You are still allowed to observe! They ram the ship,

Why not?! It's a good sport! So the weak dies. We have reserve—

Not a loss! Don't forget to wink at the boss.

In the meantime, be proud of your foxy master— She is ruse and malicious.

She'll give you a promise of what you think you want,

But that pledge is constantly delayed as you wonder why!

Meanwhile, she convinces you that she is teaching you the art of the jubilant battle—

How to serve, how to serve her purpose!

So you accept to be used in return, but why the long face?

That's why you were there in the first place.

Just sing our secretly regressive power anthem:

"Be part of the team, we tell you what you mean,

To reach that scheme, we show you what to dream.

Just trust! Trust the team, and you shall beam.

Aouuuuu- Aouuuuuu".

To entrap you, a simple plan,

She will offer you earthly pleasures—

A fragile title for your little self,

And why not a hat and custom?

"Come on and join us, be somebody." The announcement says,

Be we! Serve the inferno. Are you happy now? Not yet!

Then let's give you a special name, where everybody screams it in vain!

Captain could-be-nice! Or a bigger word—"lieutenant", maybe!

Sounds more intellectual, I know! She sniggers,

Your choice, soldier! As long as you take aim at the target we gave you—

The picture of that mother carrying her child.

You could be a medal boy, you know!

You hit the target so well!

You understand how to protect your master from that handicapped

elderly,

And her new enemies that she is planning to create—

Enemies of power, oil, drugs, arms, diamonds, you name it!

Carried by your new religion's emblem,

Conceded by your best friend's wife. Why not?!

All good! All foes in hell, all goes in hell.

Never a prisoner of virtue!

What a freedom! Freedom certainly!

Don't you need a new park, a new school and a new casino? The devil's

speech—

The inferno needs money, let's go and play—

A little campaign of fear!

Good idea, all clear.

Let them get consumed, and consume.

Yes, dear!

A war for your safety!

The treat is near.

A little genocide!

What's better than now, and here!

Out of the châteaux of hell now,

Let's plunder, ravish, and slay.

You are all dressed up for the occasion,

Clothed to impress, you are a beauty now!

You are so special! Glow upon you, wacky world!

Worth respect, and veneration, without a doubt!

No doubts in hell! All is surely hell.

And when you have to slaughter in the desert heat,

No worries! The cold blood that you shed will cool you down.

They are terrorists, don't you know?!

If you don't annihilate them, they might kill your companion of war,

While he rapes that alluring woman we saw!

We don't want that, do we?!

So let's be faster in our defence—

Kill all, let's laugh, and lighten our hearts.

What a joking joy!

Cool—cool, isn't it?

Let's drink to that.

Ah, yes! Of course! The second act—

A bottle of wine, a woman slave, and child to witness the scene.

Good show, it's a good laugh indeed.

Let the children rage, and give them guns,

Easier to shoot a "raw" on the run!

Steal their toys, and stick them on your swords—

Music to my ears! How well you play those chords!

Then let them all kill each other,

When in fury, they won't know a foe from a brother.

Call them children of the revolution.

Who cares?! It's just a name for the game,

To justify our private wealth's institution.

Raise your cups to the world's health,

And to killer babies defending their constitution.

Sunrise, a desert breeze, soldiers up—

Let's howl. The Wolf is here!

"Viva Democracy"! To better protect your home, I appear!

"The sky is the limit"! Liberty to our invasion!

Why are these natives in our way?!

Can't we plunder and exterminate in peace?

On our way, let us not precious time waste.

The studio is costly, CNN, thank us. Don't we finance your work?!

Let's eliminate the public hunger for the truth.

They can't handle it, you know! Why the contrite?!

They are better trained for a plight.

Must lie a bit to save the world— that's surely not out of your chords!

P.S. We have sent you a gift from our loot;

Open it boy! Don't be shy or frightened!

It's another wanted head, and please enjoy!

Enjoy the scene.

Oh, don't be gloomy now!

Just bait the trap, and fill the gap.

Film it—quick! From this angle slick,

It's still fresh—Do your trick!

The scent of death is still in the wind.

Oh, don't whine! They are fiends!

Good can't stand alone, you know that!

Inform your masters, the time does tick.

More to kill; must pay the bill—

Get on the phone, good can't stand alone!

All justified! Can't you see?! All that fright . . . !

Ohm…, quite a sight!

Back to the comedy show—

A bit of fantasy world to stun the day,

Where the third face is installed in place.

Numbing the idea of a helpless world on a death row!

Step nine: Oh, extravagance! You're quite costly!

Looking from the outside, I think,

It's far better to look at the facade's luxury with hope,

Yearning to pass the caution line,

Than being sustained in its finery charade looking out within desperation.

Those inner rotten selves that have been ignored for so long,

Stretching their eyes tempting a soulful smile,

Stamped with a bogus grimace that invades their cheeks;

Laughing vacantly just to make a sound,

Consoling their tale that has no ground,

But, still, they wonder, why their constant blankness remains!

Have you asked yourself!

How could an empty package serve thee?

Nourishing their stomachs, but not their souls,

Feeding their fake images, but not their acts,

Yearning for grace, but with a bad conscience!

Run to your office now; go back to the black and white board.

Take your position soldier, and pretend you're under control.

Oh, yes! You've obtained it all.

But where is that inner peace,

When you're out of the prescribed role?

Facing yourself in that ornamented mirror, you wonder,

Why did my heart become so dry and fierce?!

Freedom is definitely a gift; we disregard it in the name of need!

Aren't all new births started within?

With a promising hope, and a faithful seed?

Dreaming of that freedom's height,

Soaring in purity is high-priced indeed;

For those whom it was not given an innate angelic breed.

Step ten: Train for the show.

So to have compassion, I had to impersonate the average sheep.

Just before the demonstration, the swaggering on my knees.

The show: "What is it to be humble, and serve?"

To better understand the gruelling march of the herds.

Now I am feigning to be one with the predictable rabble,

Trying to observe my insights on the why and how.

What would I be if with them I should walk?

As an empress who filed her hopes, and feels much older.

What would I express if with them I must talk?

Console their limits! Again, in vain!

And maybe give them my shoulder!

What would I become, if on their ethics I would vow?

To mediocrity, conformity, and the golden badge! As any soldier!

Oh, boy! How the herds on their way to the fields,

Eat each other if they find no herbs.

Marching with a grin—all those gruesome teeth—

Only to advance their daggers for the raw meal!

Step eleven: Empower the average sheep!

In the cattle's gallery there's an unspoken code,

Sew me your teeth, and maybe I'll show you mine.

Or is it vice versa?

Same goal, just a different road,

Either way, what a sadomasochistic way to dine!

Each his pleasure, each his defence,

Each does what he can to avoid the trap and the fence.

And if he's powerless, and can't do,

He clings to the cut price, shoddy and cheap.

He only can afford to discourage with despair.

He criticises, and tempts to prove,

That he is, and also can dishearten and scare.

Interesting crowd! Indeed a crowd . . .!

Now I conjure up my inwardness, and realize that solitude is bliss.

When I am alone, I find the meaning—not to be rude or demeaning!

Commonly levity and envy are the exchange,

That deranged banality, and you call me strange!

A cocktail of bad will topped with viciousness cream;

From miles, I can feel their toxic, wearing scheme.

It's a long walk, but I must gather my strength to find my pure self.

This must be my best companion, besides a prayer or a fine read.

Or maybe doing what's in my power as a decent deed.

Because there are divine beings when they smile,

They lighten up the nearing sky, and that smoggy day,

The exuberant spirits, the real stars,

To them encounter, I shall long to share and thrive.

But sluggish movement, mired transportation!

Step twelve: Compassion towards mediocrity's evil and malice?!

Empathize with mediocrity!

What an unrelenting frustration!

Observing their languid faces stirred,

That fodder confused for a conversation.

The alarm triggers my coma again—not an ultimate situation.

Put my soul at risk?! What about self-conservation?

What if it's contagious? All this for a dowdy confrontation!

I have to succeed in failing to attend, from their energy field of contamination.

Just to be tied in with?! In the name of the tenure and integration!

Visiting their Lethe waters— that's surely a "no-vacation"!

All this is no spirit enhancer! But decadence to my essence's modulation!

I must stay clear, to receive heavenly information.

Maybe when I'm perfectly serene after a lifetime!

And compassion becomes my home, not destination!

I can walk on their waters, and then safely dive.

Big if, but I'll make the reservation.

As for now, if I fill my mind with their blabber and clutter,

And watch them idiotically or sneakily brawl, over status or football,

Will I have space for genuine creation?

Don't Gods create when all alone?!

In tranquil elation, observing from afar!

Roaming in heaven's globes for a fresh inspiration!

Not when enmeshed in the horrors of human deterioration!

Anyhow, I'm for most as a kid's taste of wine.

I'm not their savour, and they're not mine.

Also the best of them, for me, are as caviar.

Just for special occasions, good they are.

I just fear that with leniency, I'll lose the taste of perfection.

I must in my mind's space sit and ponder,

And deeply dig and in all dimensions trawl,

Yet sustain tolerance to heal this inherent situation.

Maybe learn to combat with kindness!

Allow my heart to see a new interpretation!

Am I also frayed by a mysterious widespread lethargy?

Good question. Quite the observation!

I shall hold onto my feast-or-famine attitude towards all,

Since the battlegrounds are stacked with mediocre soldiers.

As what is an ocean with limited waters? Freedom with one wing!

What is a morning without its wonderful promise and peace?!

Or love without admiration?! Or an evening without its joy!

You understand my connotation!

I still have a long, onerous fight.

Prepared I am, I only have to outmanoeuvre my burdened wits.

I must over myself reign, not get lost in between,

And not to conformism subdue or crawl.

I guess I lost the eyes of the child my boy,

While he watches me from within in frustration.

Squealing for liberty, love, and acceptance,

That kindness without imperious compartmentalisation.

I keep thinking I'm above all. But my head now is against the wall.

Yet hoping that beguiling portal will slide open,

Then transport my ancient soul to the enchanted garden,

To share the joy and laughter of a noble immortal, or a few, for that matter!

Magnetised by their happiness, as I stand underneath the sunny tree of life,

And witness them laugh gleefully, and bathe in rose petals attar.

But if, and when I open up, will I trigger a new answer?!

Can I train my nature the steps of a new dancer?!

Question being: Have I ever been the empathetic child?

The one who believed in innate goodness while in agony cried!

Have I ever dared to let her express what I forebode?

Being kind to a scorpion! Say no more! Ask the frog!

Upon my word! True to form a deadly code.

But again, how much more can I lay bare?!

Can my eternal soul be ever at risk? Sincerely!

Or is it my ephemeral ego that I don't like to whisk?

No, really!

And isn't it better to have tried and failed,

Than to remain tormented, besieged, and jailed?!

And can I fail in the absolute sense? Only nearly!

Wouldn't I grow and learn, now and yearly!

All this is beautiful in theory, but I must dearly practice.

Quite clearly!

Still, it's tiresome to struggle and breed the same results.

Isn't sometime time to quit, take it in vigour as perishing adults?

I keep touching the fires, and question why I got burned.

Throw myself from edges, and wonder why I can't fly.

I can swear I tried. Perhaps now, I should rest, and die.

But quite possibly,

I must persevere in my battle against my ego's lies.

Separating me that sociopath,

To have me in exclusivity, without any ties!

Murmuring to me a folly of grandeur,

That leads me to discarded goodbyes.

I must dare again to set my inner child free.

Naively not! But without fear or judgment to be!

As even if the sea doesn't fly, is it less than the bird? Isn't it also divine?

And if the talk has sound and words, is it greater than silence?

Isn't stillness its vocation?

Each his duty to complete the circle, isn't that the way of a sudden miracle?

But why all these questions, when daily we fight for a bed and bread?

Compassion is the key, the Lord has said! With boundless mercy and love!

Maybe it's true, silly of me.

But how can I give what I don't have?! That's a truth I dread.

And who would worry about all this when happy, and well fed?

Each his destiny and fulfillment— Why I may, and you mayn't?!

Must be like Gods, kind and clement! Who am I to judge?!

No grudge! Yes admiral, but no sergeant!

The way I know is to be radically alone, but you mustn't.

I'll compose my art of expression, that's what will sustain me,

In every season and every session!

And if fortunate enough,

I'll have friends in the blessed skies that will salute me,

That will be my moment!

But before that glorious instant,

I must examine my every turpitude one at a time.

That surely will come as bitterness in lime.

And if I radically change the ways of my mind,

Will I cease being ignorant and blind?

The world is in the eyes of the beholder,

Is it true because it has been said?!

So if I change my perception on the massacres, for instance,

Will they end?!

Saw the news! Have you heard?!

But first, please stay with us for a little break of advertisement.

Need a new suit! Want premium fuel! Do you like my biscuits?

Compassion please! No judgment.

Or did I project it unlawfully and meant to say,

Compassion "pleases not" judgment.

The pitiless song of war: I need beauty, I need fuel.

It's good to be the bomb in the rocket,

You're a big hit. You rule!

The death of many for the king—

He has to win the chess match.

Enemies have to die.

It's a good cause, for the people,

It can't be cruel!

It's a duel between unarmed child and a trained soldier,

It's just a game! Just a duel!

What's another child or another combatant?!

We need fuel.

Sharpen your heads, little soldiers, as you are the arrow we target with,

You are the tool!

It's "good" to end with your glorified lives,

With those joker mass-produced costumes you're wearing,

Labelled: Made in China,

But someone all dressed up told you that it's hot and cool.

What's another child, mother, or warrior?

What's the fuss? Just another mule!

Just serve me my tea. God save the king and the queen.

Hurry up, you fool!

Oh, repulse me not! Put yourself together when you see my royal biscuits,

Is that blue-collar blood you drool?!

Guillotine boy, come here!

Remove this disgusting poor creature,

What's another soldier?! I need beauty, I need fuel.

Step thirteen: Embrace the enemy!

Annexe 1: Turn the other Cheek, that's our new peek!

A question as old as water: shall we gift compassion to evil?

For sure, in the material world, a query that's not worth a quarter.

Sincere are we when compassionate towards the wicked?!

All those humanistic crimes!

Turn the other cheek! That's our new peak!

Or choosing to go along because we wish no waves!

In our perfect system of the master and the slave,

Or must we punish back to preserve the rules?!

Yes, why not be brave!

Let's test our snide dogs and set them loose.

Let them run wild, believing they wore an endless leash,

Let's see how much they'll abuse!

Maybe in their fast speed to destruction,

They'll break their own necks—those ruse!

Isn't that karma's doctrine and evident way

When we choose its morals to ignore and disobey? So what to do?!

Should we applaud and howl when they're hanged?

Or can we heal a few dark souls by seraphic edification?

Can we remedy their malign?

But what if they find ludicrous that donation!

Don't ferns flourish in the shade? Maybe a flower is not their trade!

So is it more reasonable to fine them where it hurts most?

In their pride and jewels! But that's not an innovative actuality.

Should we blind them on how they can hurt us those heartless minds?

Imprison those fools as they respect no school! Here's a revolutionary duality.

But then who will save the world? Can you tell who'll…?!

Another bites the dust! Now I'm hero for conviviality!

Why can't we develop our innate conscience simply?

Knowing that stealing their wives or bread is an act for wimps and mules.

Yes, we can . . . inflict more damage, because we are wickeder, and have more tools!

We are the wolves and they are the sheep, it's natural for us to hunt and leap.

But where does it all stop?! When we conquered the top?! And then!

Who is there left to rob? Each other! Welcome to the impious hope!

We reached the common summit—bottoms up! Hop, you trot, trot to
the top.

I am still angry at their selfish "powers" and blind greed.

Give charity to the poor, "feel better about yourself",

For what you did in the dark. Yes, that deed.

So why not donate the dime?

The promoting king, I don't deny, I his role played and did.

Attempting now, my ignorance to kill and rid.

Sometimes I know I'm the biggest fool of them all,

And if at last I found the key, why can't I put it on the roll?

Possibly it's just me—oh, that redemption!

I can't forgive myself, so how can I forgive thee?!

So I hold myself in isolation, in retention.

Trying to obtain a quiet mind, a refuge of peace!

Longing for a state of grace, but alas, for that motionless pace!

Trapped I am as I abhor unrefined conventions.

But have to meet it, no remedy, and no prevention.

I block my memory till I reach blankness,

In that absolute oblivion, deterring my mind till self-treason,

Fearing to be reminded of my omnipresent torment,

And of my past existence that was so disgruntled, unfulfilled, and thankless.

I must stay still now and relax;

I think my karma already paid its tax.

Perhaps if we all understood joy and beauty,

Then we all choose peace!

If we stop edging, burdening, and judging one another,

We'll stop buying life and putting ourselves on the lease.

Not a revolution what I call for.

But to love oneself, that's already one more!

I must begin with my own unconditional love,

And not one silver hair shivers me; to be clear, my hair above.

Maybe their noise and clamour is from within!

I have to live with the place where I hide;

And not in constant friction with my own skin!

So present for them I am, but where is my reflection?!

And absent me is absent God, whether in a palace, or in a combative squad.

But does that explain the insignificance I persistently ride?

Does it justify my baffled intentions?

So much left to discover and understand,

If only I encounter my inner guide!

In my past, happiness—with money, I tried to buy it.

I listened carefully to how they described it.

I tried to kill that numbing pain, with credit cards—I'm not to blame!

To their pinnacle I reached, but none of it fits,

Money will sell you out if you don't buy it.

That's what's in the money, that's what's in the wealth.

Paid by your soul, peace of mind, and health!

Not only my daemons must I face,

But also the evil in others marked in the quotidian trace.

Those inferiors playing superiors,

Exasperated, why they're thwarted,

Yet, you, the foreign nature are at peace?

So bitterly, they accuse you of lack of propriety,

As you don't join in, in their thespian piece!

Tolerance my soul, tolerance!

Be still my heart, rage not now, stay cool,

This can't be the hopeless case!

Be serene and wait for enlightenment.

Oh, that eternal strenuous transformation!

Not from wild dogs to driven cattle,

But to the God within,

That can bring loving light to this endless battle.

Annexe 2: Handle the liars. Oh, how I love you!

He starts by observing you well;

To study you better, know your Achilles' heel.

He pretends to care about your secret desires,

Not out of liking,

But to better take aim at what you feel.

He asks you a thousand questions,

But better not ask him any.

He makes you believe you're in control,

When lives, he manipulated many!

What is missing in your life? Tell me, girl!

What you desire most, I can promise you, my pearl!

No unattainable wish for you and "I",

We can strive and long for all,

Would I lie?!

He knows what makes you keen, he gets under your skin,

Under your habits and weak addictions,

Trying to obscure your intuition, till you are tender and lean!

When you are ripe and feeble, he seduces and presents the deal:

"Oh, baby, this feels so right, I feel so happy and all is real,

And tomorrow we'll have our fortune wheel."

When you realize his empty promises, he has no more cards to deal.

He takes his distance and hides, to better manipulate you, to operate his zeal.

Now you feel you need him as a fix;

And all your being trembles and in itself mix.

Unreasonable you were, and pushed him away;

You are crazy, and your needs are surreal.

Meanwhile, you sexily pause on your crucifix,

While you rot, what a fine seal!

When you least expect him, he returns,

Crying, pleading, claiming his need is forever real.

That's why he was there in the first place,

To help you share that ideal!

So he with a glance screams, begs, and kneels:

"Oh, darling, how I miss you, love you, will never leave you!

Take me back, let me save us, let me save you,

I'll answer all your questions, I'm no eel!"

A break from your cross, you think.

He hugs you before you can blink.

Then he swears there's a better tomorrow,

To give him enough time to take and borrow.

To ravish your being, better your life to steal,

To lease your blood, so he can heal.

You now begin to realize, it's time to close your heart and open your eyes.

You planted a manipulative grain in your secret garden,

You planted that poisonous herb, that bad seed!

You invited him under your loving tree, and when you shift your head,

He buries you underneath it, and sing a love song to his new invitee,

In your garden he nests—this pest—above your grave, he sips your

afternoon tea.

Annexe 3: Manipulating the manipulator! Bye, love.

One too many crafty liars, and addicted you become,

To the rush and its anguish, to find the one!

To manipulate a manipulator, listen with care.

To their parting pretext, the rehearsed text!

With wild flowers in his hands, he declares:

"I don't want to hurt you, darling, but I must cut and run.

Don't condemn me, just yet! And don't you, please, jump the gun!

You would have been bored with me!

You need much more than the sun.

And when we shared a family dream,

You chose a cat over a son!

Our home we had, as we played,

Together we built it on a clear day.

Remember! It was on the sand!

But, still, my love, you have won!

You know you never intended to stay.

Just be positive, babe, we had lots of fun,

Stare at the stars, forget the mud.

Only in stars hearts don't change,

Magnetic you were, but not the one!

Our moments, in our memories will remain,

And the best love stories never last!

Spring is precious because it's just a season,

And we were once, and once, you were my reason.

I was there to awaken your heart,

And, that honey, is no treason!"

Did I push him to the goodbye?! He made me believe!

Is that how much I love my freedom? Or simply he wanted to leave!

Am I just comforting my soul? For knowing my destiny is so lonesome!

I shall mourn for losing the magic in my random streets,

As when he held my hand in his, I felt that I held the world.

Oh, my pain! Rise above my shielded sheets!

As in the game of love, I'd rather lose,

To evade succumbing to its hell!

As my beaten heart became just news;

But in one blessed morning, I'll heal well!

Farewell my heart, farewell my handsome!

Annexe 4: The love songs series / Breakup number 1

23rd of December 2007

How could you leave me in a sudden night?

To myself to greet me every night!

When I knew love and tenderness in your arms,

My face in my pillow; only darkness in sight.

I bury my thoughts, and tell myself "just another bastard."

But, baby, for the love of the game,

We know, that my heart, you have mastered.

I thought I found you, but you had to push me away.

Love is too much for you, you had to lead us astray.

The hope I had to love again is gone,

The spark I guarded for the one is done.

Put flowers on my tomb, baby, I thank you indeed.

Somehow, you know exactly what I need.

You fear love more than you fear life,

That explains the stab in my back. What a lovely sharp knife!

Let's walk dead and walk blind. The point, darling, let's lay aside.

Let's say goodbye as we said hello,

Strangers in the night not knowing friend from foe!

Annexe 5: *Every victory is just a mile* / Breakup number 2

15th Novemeber 2007

I'm on fire, and it's 35 degrees outside.

My only desire is an angel with a mysterious ride.

You tell me: "Baby,

Just come on and wear a smile."

I tell you: "Maybe,

Every victory is just a mile."

You tell me: "Lady,

Walking on the edge is a dangerous line!"

I tell you: "Maybe,

What's a man without a passionate spine?"

You tell me: "Shady,

Loving your risk might wear you out!"

I tell you: "Maybe,

That's a chance I won't go without."

You say to me: "Start and seek (vis à vis),

Stop dreaming and be pragmatic."

I tell you: "Can't you see?!

A life without a dream is just haemostatic."

You tell me: "Baby,

You're building a galaxy on a sandy mansion!"

I tell you: "Maybe,

But life without risk is love without passion."

You say to me: "Darling,

Stop "you" going to extremes."

I tell you startling,

"Can you ask a river not to stream?!"

I tell you: "Baby,

Let it go, I'm going my own way,

And surely maybe, no matter what you say, I won't sway."

You tell me: "Okay, can't handle your euphoric swings,

So it's time baby to give me back my diamond ring!"

Annexe 6: I hate you, my love. Breakup number 3.

18th of June 2006

I hate you my love, I hate my pain.

I hate you, and that's now all what's main.

When I see you, I long for your arms in… in vain.

Oh fade away—I can't see you, and pretend that I'm the same!

You pass by me, and pretend not to see me! What's your game?!

Just walk away and disappear, I have no more heart in me to burn.

With all my lovers of the past! Oh! My lesson, I did learn!

Your teeth are marked upon my soul! It's my essence you just stole!

I'll stay alone, it is better that way. With time, I'll convince myself, that you were gay!

And now, that you're gone, I'm all alone. Sitting helpless by a silent phone!

I have no cigarettes. The shops are closed. The night is long. The stars are cold.

Annexe 7: Phoenix! Chocolate cake, or die for a while!

I just wanted to die for a while, shy for a while!

Wonder on the nothing, empty my pain, and be reborn again!

Phoenix, question! Did life give me life to live it, or serve it?

And do I serve it by living a loving reason?

But no matter what it is that I lived for,

I dared to take thousand doors; and with this last door,

I'll rise above my ashes, collect what's left me and throw my hatches.

No more winding to get to aim, it dulls me now to manipulate the game.

Purify me, crucify me! Love is like youth, ephemerally vain!

Annexe 8: Fool me once

So strong you are, and you rise above your loss,

Hurting, knowing you've been deceived.

A dire lesson for a better march,

Leaned on the wrong wall, played the wrong ball!

Finally, you weren't the boss.

Some you care about but they don't go for the kill;

They just go when they lose the thrill.

So time to rise above the self- inflicted pain, and heal.

Knowing, this chapter must now seal.

Safe you are, and you forget that once he had torn you asunder,

As his hello in the distance sounds tender, and sweet!

Longing for that ardent heat, as the sure sounds in a maddened thunder!

You let him in, again,

To realize that you only yourself comfort, but cheat!

A sweet and sour defeat!

In the face of a lover, friend, or helper they appear,

But they are loathers of themselves and others,

So be warned of their smoke…!

They want you numb. A glass of rum!

Drug addicts, suicides, chronic liars,

Or indigent little spirits, attention whores, any buyers?!

Antagonists indeed, foes with silk veils,

Appearances and false promises are their weapons,

That to you they'll never reveal.

They invite you for a delicious dinner to cook you under low fires,

Marinating you sumptuously, yum- yum- to become the meal.

Annexe 9: A love beyond. I don't stand in queues.

I'll have a love beyond reason, logic, or time.

Beyond comfort, fashion, and crime—

A love that stands the darkest nights.

Beyond fear and hesitation, that feels just right.

I'll have a love from the first glance,

That gaze which breathes and has no doubt.

Just in passion and needs no why,

A love without shame, or need to blame.

I'll have a love that I do lust,

Yet trust and respect are my musts.

No matter where he is or I,

I walk with peace of mind.

Alone he travels his journey sometimes,

While I walk in joy's pride.

And when he's back and his eyes in mine,

He takes me on a thousand ride.

I'll have a love that shouts my name,

Not when I'm poor or rich in fame.

A love that sings and dances,

Wouldn't that be a joyous chance?

I'll have a love that dares the magic nights,

And allows me to fly to the highest heights.

A love that knows and simply shows,

A love that streams and in life flows.

Not let's see! That's so lame.

At least a clever line, before you throw me in the rain!

I know you don't love me, I'm not that vain.

So go, babe, go your way.

Why compromise? I won't sway.

Goodbye now, go find your one.

My love for you is so done.

I threw it up with your deceiving news,

Oh, not me, who'll stand in queues.

Annexe 10: Feel the love! Go home to daddy . . . cool.

I've been gone long ago,

All alone in a silly world.

I've been searching for love,

Taking the long way home.

Found instead of love, pain.

Maybe I lost my main!

I'm coming home.

Yes father, I'm coming home.

I see the flag,

Roaming the desert land,

Saluting me, praising my tears.

But when I get there,

Will you meet me and open the door?!

To set me free

From my memories

That won't let me be!

I know you're deceived I ran away,

But father, I just couldn't stay—

All that violence and endless threats,

On my life you always bet.

I'm here now admiring the scene,

In your white gown, you don't seem so mean.

So will you meet me halfway,

I'm crying climbing the stairs?!

Take me in your arms,

Nothing remained.

No, I'm not dead father.

Say your hello and your goodbye,

And when it's time for me to go,

I want to depart with tears, but walk tall.

Years have passed and I still try,

To forget all my childhood.

I became soulless and blind,

Lost on a one-way street.

Will you forgive me for not knowing how to love?!

Will you accept me even if my crest is not the dove?

Truly, I want to take you in my heart,

But these chains keep us so apart.

Father, you can't cry my tears,

Nor mend my aching heart,

Nor soothe my pain,

Nor give me peace,

You can only love me as I love thee.

So will you please set me free?!

So I learn for once just to be!

Liberate me, father!

P.S. I love you very much, and always will. Forgive me for choosing my own way!

Annexe 11: Nefarious rivalry

Children of war, sleep, babies, sleep!

There's a hole in the sky, it's an eye to heaven. I lie;

To the children that must die,

It will take you higher, I comfort, but in silence I cry.

How much dying do we still need?!

How much suffering do we have to breed?!

In the name of God! Or in the name of need!

I won't stand still, and see you kill.

And . . . there's a hole in the sky . . .

Time again for the comedy show,

Where more masks than I care to admit are stuck in my frozen face!

Maybe a bit of sun will be appropriate now, a tan for my flaking soul.

Yes, I shall go to that happy place, where heaven validates its heavenly grace.

When the sun beams with its heavenly kiss, in that garden of the eternal

bliss!

Good, the morning and the mailman are here—

A letter for me! Titled: Dear Mother!

Maternity I never knew, no children of mine!

"Open it, girl! Don't be shy or frightened!

And please enjoy, enjoy the read!"

It reads: *Dear Mother,*

In the line of fire I stand,

Poor, naked, and unarmed!

From my freedom, I'm banned.

With my hand, my head I cover.

Injured, bleeding dragging my brother.

Barefoot among mines, I run.

Do I have time to shudder?!

In the line of fire I stand,

Shall I die today Mother?!

In the name of God, we kill!

In the mire, His name we smother.

I raise my "arms" to that stranger,

Who wears my two thousand years jewels;

He stole from me, and raided my home,

In the name of a claim, as the holy heir!

While the airspace was hailing fire!

In that one moment, we stood, and stared at each other.

Yes, that mirrored fool!

He was my brother; wasn't he Mother?!

Selling himself in the media as the victim!

First a vicious echo of the Oriental music,

Then, the sad peaceful other!

Would you advise me, Mother?!

Must I donate my heart to my brother so he can heal?

And does that mean that one must die for the other to live?

Who would benefit from all that?! Who wants us to extinct each other?!

The ones who feed on our wars, I suppose!

Those kind men, which for our coffins prepared a rose!

Angels! Evil is like disease, unjustly spreading!

How can I help in ceasing prejudice, violence and hate?!

How can we heal so we can start to love?!

"Forgive what you think you can't", she softly said,

"Vengeance is eternal hate; you mutually caused the innocent deaths,

And you both claim "your rights" in land, and carnage!

While "public servants" sell the divine's land to the highest bidder,

Their hearts shades are shut in darkness, so why reconsider?

They free the famished from life with a vampire's dish,

So they can dig rivers for their incarcerated fish!

No more space for another coffin, there is a flood.

How can man rest in peace when he is buried in blood!

Hiding the atrocities under the holy name! Shame!

This vicious circle of brutality must now end,

It is only love that can salvage.

Go back within, and quietly listen,

And for goodness sake, just be a lover.

Now, open your eyes, and remove that cover.

Both pains, I admit, are timeless.

But naming a race as the holy heir!

While one blows up, and the other goes off!

Meanwhile, compassion causes a scoff!

Oh, this ignorance, my heart can't bear!

Forgive the unforgivable! Will you try?

Help them redeem their dignities, and pride.

Vanquishing the other is a losing combat.

Because one will reign, and that is love,

Maybe for now this is just a dream,

But didn't God start the world like that!

We must feed the goodness before it's too late!

The evil shout shall be famished,

As no place in heavens for porters of hate!"

Oh, Mother!

Heaven is not simple! But I'll try to be humble!

And attempt to comprehend and heal, as I discover.

Annexe 12: Change, come to me, do not shame!

August 2006

Time to return, and sit under the antediluvian banyan tree,

And talk to the life force of spiritual enlightenment.

Maybe a bit of retreat will guide me!

To find a way to be forgiven,

For all I manoeuvred to be given.

And for my pledges that I have riven!

Why was I so mercilessly driven?!

But there isn't anyone beyond reproach,

And that is my comfort.

So if you judge me now, hold your stones,

Let's compromise with another approach!

Maybe, you would like a carrot!

Didn't you once have the horse sense aim?

The sense of: What's in today?! What's in its gain?!

Oh, stoical existence! Why did you allow such harmful creations?

So you can become the hero, and our savior?!

Why so lame, and why so vain?!

Yes, I had to lose all to find my essence.

But if I die now,

Will anyone care to frame my picture, or simply miss my presence?

My tears are stuck behind my shunned echoes!

Will some God release the rain?!

Oh, my dear spirit, did I overplay my hand searching for you?

And did I ever care to tame? Wild, I remained, safer that way!

No, not I, who'll need a fallible love! And what for!

So I can stare at another who babes his name!

Oh, my unprepared spirit, be kind now!

As no card left to trade! My last ace I have laid.

What have I done?! What have I made?!

Say hello to your winter season, my dear self!

It came in a sudden and in a rush,

I didn't even have time to realize my ageing face!

Is this sneaky arrival my sorrowful end?

This ferocious storm deracinates an ancient tree!

Adieu, my noble pride that I must rend!

"But do not fear my soul! A clear whisper in my head:

Protected you are by the eternal hearts." She said:

"You know that the Almighty has His reasons,

And every kingdom will face its treason.

Maybe, the fall is ineludible now,

To develop compassion for those who crawl!"

Oh, whisper! Dear whisper!

Thank you for sharing the heart of this trauma,

But I won't turn my life to drama! I'll have my heaven,

Where heaven is love and love is my heaven.

I just have to climb through those Penrose steps!

Till I find sky number seven.

Dear Lord! I'm really grateful for my height!

Tall you've made me, closer to you to nest and be!

But my head is in the skies, and my feet on the grounds!

What a human excrescence!

And if I could choose wings over roots,

I would forever in the sky stay.

But for now, I must face the harvest of my credulous mistakes!

I'm in a perishable sight, and travel within vague transportation!

Wondering, if I'll I suffer as much if in the wilderness I lived!

But wherever I run, captive to my delicate conscience, I remain.

Till, everlasting freedom announces to be.

Oh epiphany, Oh enlightenment!

Can't you see that I'm in shame?

Trying to find someone to blame,

My heart no longer has a flame,

Alive or dead is just the same.

Step fourteen: Where is that treasure? Where is my Supreme?

I convince myself to keep going, just one more mile,

The fight is almost over, but the breakthrough is so out of my reach!

Just one glimpse of its light's perfection, please!

While I climb that supreme humbling road, I silently roar:

Where is that treasure?! Why is that absolute need?!

Maybe a too-good-to-be-true promise is far better than an irksome pleasure!

I persist, that is the warrior's way of life, conquer or die trying!

To perfect the central call, that timeless seed,

That dedicated cause in the heart.

Some are the shell, and some are the pearl.

Certain to protect, and certain the treasure to breed.

I'm crossing those pitiless deserts with this gruesome camel beast.

To reach the heart of the divine, that oasis, the fresh start,

Which is unreachable by a human pass, but maybe by his centre and soul!

This creature's invisible wings are the heavenly dragon,

Sending me to protect its earthly paradise,

Is that why I seemed so mean?

Would a lion be king if he looked so lean?!

Or God be as real if he could be seen?!

Yes compass, I follow you. My road diverges to west, not east!

To this open market where dreams are for sale, where I'll buy another dream.

To be blessed, devout yet free, not crucified and nailed!

I'm walking my path with a kind heart and a holistic claim.

No matter what and when, I'll get to my aim.

But darn it! Will I ever truly live a Utopian celebration?

When is that reward?! And what is a feast?!

Without strain and onus's iteration!

And if in that halo I'm summoned,

Will heaven's doors welcome me with my beast?

For now, I must wander alone.

Friends, I had a few—those who came and went.

Some lived to the fullest, but died young,

I'm hoping immortal love to them was sent.

So a red rose I threw over each corpse of my priests,

In their beauteous youth, the scent of death plucked their perfume!

And some had angelic faces, but only complained and wept,

If they could feel a ray of sun, at least!

Or admit that it's natural for a spring to bloom!

As for me, I journey with a spirit for any ache,

No fear to put all at stake,

With a head high and I know why,

Yet puzzled I don't deny!

That's the life of an artiste.

And when I review my dreams in my bed,

I may feel that I regret,

But none of that, not this bro,

That much I do know.

As I am daring all before I'm dead,

With a wondering soul that leads the way,

With a grateful heart for every day.

Criticized I am for my risky bays,

And for riding life in unconventional ways.

But my every stop is to cleanse and learn,

How to tolerate what I'd rather burn.

A story I do have to tell,

As I carried my banners out of hell.

I lived as fully as I could,

I didn't do the musts and "shoulds".

But still, time sinks its fangs in my esprit de corps,

Withal, agnostic forces are draining me,

And they think they know what's for.

Lonely shadows projecting their wraith,

Planting apprehension where there is faith;

With their gloomy hearts, never gay,

Blaming others, even for May.

No, none of that—I shall take no more,

Even their breath is a serious bore,

Oh God no! Needless to say!

How can I be in when I want out?!

How can I live in faith when all is doubt?!

How can I maintain peace with their inner shout?!

Angels, quiet, please!

A stillness sound maybe!

My ears in the seas, my eyes on the skies,

My cheeks kissed by the loving sun,

My arms laid aback in the cool blue,

Floating in perfect harmony with this hot summer breeze,

Surfed by heavenly creatures to my blessed new home;

Meanwhile, asked if any needs—

Yes, please, that's so nice! Just a cocktail, thanks, no cheese.

But cut—

Angels, questions please: Do you ever weep?!

Do you ever have burden and grief?

Or did God give you that zenith belief?

Will you give me an example of that heavenly leap?!

And when addressed with incessant despair, don't you fade a bit?

How does your light stay lit?!

How can you still be love and light?

How can I find my blithe and delight?

That timely action, when to discard and when to keep!

Only to you can I turn, only for you do I wish to yearn,

Or am I just a rapid robot waiting for my serving sheep?

My heart was a rebellion, and now I wonder,

Where is my strength that with its glance my enemies fled?

When fear feared me.

Where is that inspirer in me that taught death life?

Now, there's no life in my living?! Just, dissonance and strife!

I was lit with inward glee,

Today, gaiety whiffs me and flees!

Where is my will that broke stone?

And when from the impossible I usurped the throne.

Now, I compromise and plead!

Oh, unknown, what's your creed?!

Is it to know suffering that I must suffer!

And must I embrace a chapter as the meek?

To have compassion for the weak!

Yes, my rivals! At last, my dress is torn.

Gloat away, and show your teeth. I won't break them today!

Enjoy your moment, it won't last.

Go ahead! Attack me while I'm sedated with pain!

Why not also salt my wounds! And haul me as you please—

Oho, how you can lead! But, wail not when I wake!

I pity you, but I shall not scorn.

My inner pride, no need to loathe! Oh, no need.

Step Fifteen: Thank you for leaving

Annexe 1: Leeloo is hiding behind me / a dialogue between me and my ego!

I remember, sometime ago, I dreamt

That my inner monster was getting bored.

I, holding back that poisonous arrow, hindered him,

To wander, aim at his quarry, and capture their scent!

He said, "What happened to our shared love we adored?"

I replied in faith, "I let go, fierce spirit; go find another soul to rent."

"Just wait, my heart," he said:

"Where're you going?! Just come back here.

You think you're leaving! Suddenly you're clear!

Let me remind you, babe, without me, you're just an ape.

You'll make no money! Face it, honey!

Let's discuss, create no fuss!

I'm your real companion,

I'm your hope; I'm your stallion.

Don't try to defy me, dear.

This is the rule, don't be a fool!

You're under stress, no need to press,

No panic, baby! I'm under control.

Just relax now, let's have a ball.

I'll make us number one, as I always did!

We're on the roll, we're in the bid.

Ah, in your Chanel dress! You look like Bes!

I must confess you stand so lovely and tall!

But to keep it all, you must listen and obey.

But now, lie on my silk veil if you must, come—just lay.

I'm here to guide you—bitter to swallow!

I'll show you the way, you just follow!

I've been with you forever!

Why did you keep me so long if without me you're terribly clever?!

Think again—you need me now,

Leaving me is incredibly wrong.

You believe you want to run! But, baby, I'm your shadow,

I'm your Santa, I'm your blow! HO HO HO!

Without me, there's no fun!

Now come here, and give me a kiss!

I'm your protector, I'm your bliss.

Now hush, my girl, you know I love you.

You are my one, my only Dis."

"Are you done now?!" I think.

So I chanted back to my inner foe:

"Much obliged to your cogent, pithy speech!

Would you like with that a whiskey or a peach?

Now silence my boy, I shall speak,

After all, you're not so chic!

I'm not you, I can sense you coming,

You just keep me confused and numbing.

I take my control back, and command you to snooze.

With that, like a pill with some booze!

I can perceive your babble now.

Oh, not that repulsive vow!

Go now, go your way.

Oh, how you led me astray!

You outstayed your welcome,

Staring in my mirror playing handsome.

Whirring in my head your pains and fears,

No more feeding on my tears,

Adding layers on my years,

I'm passing your limit,

I'm crossing your line,

I do not fear, it is my time.

My blade will stay covered in its sheath,

No heads will roll on my streets.

No longer need to win the game, or anyone to defeat—

By legitimate effort, or by canny cheat.

Now hit the road but not on my feet.

How I've had it with your deceit!

A trophy for your lies!

The most credible I've ever heard.

Or was it the truth that I never dared?!

But now, I can stare your devil straight in the eye,

Shame for you, I've grown out of dread, dear.

Problem there with your hell!

Goodbye now, protect it well.

Manage without me, I need what's true.

I stand alone, no need for you."

Yes, he left me, indeed!

I was discarded without a noble temper,

Wondering how to be armed with pureness and goodness!

How to fight without fury, position, and wealth?!

I thought I'd search the answer within a soul's journey—

Oh that road has much length!

I'm still disoriented and bemused, but, now also, frail and bleak.

While he sneers his "fare hell" at me,

In tears, I sensed him leave.

He knew better not to come back,

And I knew better not to look back.

Annexe 2: Penury, hello!

In life's streets I remain,

Seeing souls, examining pain.

How did I judge?! Oh, how vain!

I thought I knew, but I had no clue;

I believed in their eyes, that trite fame.

Repenting time in the mouths of snakes,

So tall I am, they just chewed my name.

Sucking my blood—vampire's shake!

For God's sake, I'm in the make

Of a new spirit, of a new dame.

Conclusively, I am hungry and sad,

But strangely purified and glad.

As I was examining my ways,

All thought I'm strange and mad.

Yes, I grew but not in stealth,

I earned all my inner wealth.

I dared to explore my every me,

I'm humbly proud of what I dare to see.

I threw myself in the arms of life,

She opened her heart to my inner strife.

She treated me mystifier than fiction,

Miraculously helping my deep friction.

I feel new as a newborn,

But this time, the queen would like her throne.

No more a flower with a thousand thorn,

I want to surrender to love and light,

As angels without restrictions.

To that perfection, I will reach—

Something I know I must teach.

But now, I'm searching my unconscious self,

Lost and poor without a compass,

But to my lord, I'm much obliged to beseech.

Step sixteen: Hey God, do you see me in the dark here?!

Annexe 1: Are you there?!... 1st of August 2007

In my silence, I talked to God:

When did I start to walk an empty dream?!

Everything is not what it used to seem.

I was rich, now I'm poor!

I was proud, now I'm humble with no scheme!

I am ashamed of walking that stream.

I hurt no one, but my pockets are empty,

I have no job, nor does my life have a theme!

So tell me, lord!

Where's my courage?

Where's my will?

Where's my aim?

Where's my whim?

Tell me!

Why am I dead when I'm alive?!

Why am I so weak when I used to strive?!

Why am I so lost when I used to guide?!

Where's that flame I used to ride?!

Tell me!

Why does love keep evading me?!

In the arms of a lover I have to flee!

Why do I feel so mad?!

How did I become so waned and sad?

Tell me!

Do you want me kneel?!

To scream a voice I have no longer?

To stand! When I cannot pretend to be any stronger?

I'm tired of fighting,

Exhausted of restarting,

Dulled with trying,

Sometimes of living!

Did you forget me? Did you?! Forget me?

Tell me!

Will you show me the way in this dark paradise?!

When do you carry me home!

Can you give me life and not freeze my soul?!

When do you carry me home!

Will you awaken my passion to long again?!

When do you carry me home!

Can I kill my daemons and still stand tall?!

When do you carry me home!

Will you find me a reason?

A love without treason!

A man I can cherish!

And let my sadness perish!

Tell me!

In a dream, a whisper, a sign, a breeze!

Why am I dead when I'm alive?

Why am I so weak when I used to strive?

Why am I so lost when I used to guide?

Where's that flame I used to ride?

Tell me!

Annexe 2: Vomit my terror!

I hope before my last curtain falls,

I'll be kinder, purer, and saner.

I'm tired. Did I just wake up or am I now going to sleep?

I must make a stop now to vomit my terror;

So the next day I can vanquish another monster, pirate, or serpent,

Until I can see beyond the fear.

Looking out on the distant horizon with a glimpse of hope,

Wondering what's left to discover and enjoy,

In the hidden galaxy, filled with heavenly creatures, wonders, and magic!

Meanwhile, believing that the lord will provide all, for this

divine exploration.

For now, pertinaciously, I settle for the next season or the next land;

As I search through the snow for the first signs of daffodils

Annexe 3: The plant of miracle is ready to blossom a white flower!

Hope is back on the horizon.

In the blink of an eye after all this mess,

Greens are sprouting through years of winter—

Almost a decade of decay and death—

To hand me finally to gestation and rebirth,

To nirvana, to the empyrean myth.

So ready I am for life, with this fresh coloured dress—

Such a reviving sight! Oh, God bless.

So the question was, will I make it through!

I'll let you guess—

Right you are! Of course, a yes!

Not only will I make it, I'll have my press.

I'll sail through heaven, won't settle for less.

So it's a bit hard, yes—some stress,

But I'll pull it through with true success.

Wait and see! I trust in miracles, I must confess.

Step seventeen: Rest when you must

Spring is always generous with hope,

To its challenging beauty, and this clandestine bliss,

I'd like to cope. But the ultimate rescue is yet far,

The answer is maybe in my wishing star.

I must rest my racing face to age and wonder,

While waiting for the perfect that never comes,

Not even sure what it is in this ceaseless thunder!

And if I meet it, will I prosper or blunder?!

It's a damn long night.

I have to dream of that happy place,

Where I grow somehow fonder.

Where I hold the sun and do not burn,

When I'm the light, yes, it's my turn.

But broken I am, sad yet eager,

Filled with hope, faith, and idealism in a monstrous world.

Getting more rapidly to the wrong destination is not my purpose.

Shame on me now if I continue to swim in my vicious circle's heat!

I am buying myself a single ticket out of hell,

I wonder how much I'll miss that superfluous beat!

I no longer want to reside between my selves and in-between,

This emotive addiction to conflict is not a treat.

Step eighteen: Reside within serendipity

26th of June 2007

Your soul is drawn upon your face,

And my destiny is written upon my name.

"The flawless hope" is its meaning.

It held me straight when I felt like leaning.

The "Concha," a secret name I gave myself,

That knowing, which I don't know why and since when.

Years later, I understand that the conch is I, that white pearl,

Concealed in its inner colour and treasure.

That speech's jewel and code I must transmit.

Its mystical shell's ear ticking from beyond,

Its belling in my heart's knowledge, to portray those unvoiced words.

My shell was the armour protecting my seed,

The potential of the right understanding of opulence and beauty.

Aphrodite, I was unaware when I asked you

If you were the shell of my celestial dew!

But to see the mystery that you are smiling at,

I must find the sound of my higher truth!

My spiritual expansion and growth!

That wish upon the moon was a silent prayer,

The spiral point, the first drop of water,

That led me to my evolutionary cycle,

To merging, and union with my deep knowing.

OMMMM, the first sound that my shell produces,

Now, I know why it's humming in my head!

It's calling me home, to the lasting warmth.

I'm ready now to transpierce my odyssey,

Even if it means the death of all I once knew and was.

I know where to go now—

To find the lost beatitude in the depth of light.

Chapter 4

The Doorkeeper

Annexe 1: Qualifications please!

Walking towards the ticket booth,

"Hello, ticket maker."

"Where are you heading?" He inquires.

"I wish to journey towards the light, please!" I answer with hope.

"Are you qualified for the journey?" He asks.

"Please present your legitimate passport and valid visa." He commands.

Oh, that recurring nightmare…!

Did I forget my passport?! Again?!

Do I have a passport, or a visa?

"Yes, sir," I reply faking assurance;

"I'm qualified, but in human land they give no visas to exiles."

"I see," he responds in an attentive, ironic way.

"If exceptionally I allow you to pass, where will you be staying?"

"In inner peace, and love when I find it."

"Who is hosting the event?"

"My earth, universe, and heavenly angels."

"Did you travel alone?"

"Without a shadow, gracious creature, from darkness till dawn."

"Do you have an invitation?"

"Yes, but it's invisible to the two bare eyes;

I'm sure you've seen one of those before, sir!"

But he's not buying, and I'm not shying.

"Just let me go, I beg you," in a soundless, frustrated scream, I stare.

But he stares fearlessly back, and solicits:

"This is no playground, child of life.

Now if you can assume what you presume, tell me:

Are you aware of the consequences of your reverie?

What can you afford to lose for such a journey?

What are you willing to give up for the freedom of a footloose nomad?

How long will you be attracted to such a life?

Do you have it in you to face the expedition's acute inconveniences?

Let me hand you the itinerary, if you will:

First days, you will be faced with loneliness, sadness, weakness,

Then helplessness, followed by a collapsing depression;

'Not to be taken with alcohol.'

A few months later, even years, while enjoying the above,

You will find yourself in poverty, insecurity, and utter instability.

In the mid of oceans, you will find yourself struggling for endurance,

Bathing in typhoons, and if fortunate, sometime a sunlit breeze;

Friends from heaven might sustain you,

But your faith must be powerful and the world can tease.

You shall not doubt even while drowning,

Do you have that unconditional belief?!

You will be whipped for that unseen vision,

Humiliated, and called vicious names.

While you travel your own way,

They all live the same routine of the day.

You will even be more apart,

Confused with a rejected heart.

And in your journey, you'll receive a thousand stones,

Venomous arrows from their eyes to your bones.

Killing your daemons is your greatest self-oaths,

Finding yourself naked without your ghosts,

Sacrificing your dark force,

Praying to the true light source,

To find your reason, to find your course.

Faith, little flower! Do you have its roots?

Hope, delicate soul! Is it still etched in your name?

No more lusting after the trivial,

You are standing in the quadrivial.

Up or down? East or west?

Make your choice! Be my guest!

Are you sure it's self-conquest that you're after?

And it's not your quibbling self that is the drafter?

If confident, are you still eager to go?

When do you want to leave?

Are you ready now?!"

Too many questions doorkeeper, damn it!

Stop heckling me! Too much for my weary, brittle mind!

This eclipse has outstayed its purpose,

I can hear the darkness capering around me.

Just let me pass please! Then leave me alone! I need light!

I have nothing left here. Goodnight.

Let me go to sleep to dream of the other world, I sense,

But a response, I astonish myself and utter:

"Right you are, Mr. Persecutor, I have no a defence to present.

But can I maybe bribe you with a potential thorny crown in the skies?

Or, that, you might resent!

More veneration perhaps, or is it statistical proof you need?

Or simply a new house with a translucent roof, do I mislead?

Oh, come on now, let me through.

I'm really tired, don't be aloof!"

But he is brooding through me in stillness,

And who said silence is consent!

Not so many people travel this road and subsist,

But me in agony, I know,

It's time for one of my steps with the natural extension.

In the gates of crossroads I stand,

Not knowing where to go.

I'm just certain that I have to leave my present place and ways.

But He is holding me the wrong way,

He is holding me back.

Annexe 2: Platinum gateway

31st of July 2008

Or was it I? Clinging to my survival holding myself back!

I saw a fortified platinum gate sliding in the midst of deserts shutting.

So I ran to the magical door leading to the world beyond,

Yearning to get to the other side,

Still wondering, what does a gate stand for in the midst of nowhere?!

Suddenly I heard a soundless, loving voice screaming,

Stop! Don't you cross that line!

My mind now knows I have nothing to lose;

Why not run to the unknown new world?

But I had to listen, I always trusted that utter.

The last bit of exit is closing, sliding against my thin garments and skin!

As I let my face touch that metallic steel, I felt I had to glance in,

To see what it is that the voice is protecting me from.

And there were dozens of hungry wolves, roaring, inviting me in.

Annexe 3: The key

While praying for that door to open,

My angels were guarding the key.

Searching for joy, at least I found me.

I thought the secret was behind that gate!

Oh, how seductive was the bait!

Complete I must feel, but at what rate!

Waiting for my eternal light;

But to reach it, mustn't run, no more flight, I'll stand and wait.

I just hope while learning patience, it won't become too late.

I'll find my way—isn't it innate?

Doesn't the closed bud, in its season, show its magnificent fate!

Isn't it sometimes the delay which is the masqueraded bliss?

And the patient waiting that makes the best of meals!

Or that forced rest that allows the wound to heal.

When you lose your keys, for example,

When in a hurry to leave the house,

And you just miss that bus that was going to hit you.

Yes, that key that you take for granted!

That should be in your pocket, purse, or on the kitchen table,

Which grants you the visa of your daily ins and outs.

Without it, you will not pass through the closed door,

May it be money, love, pride, or faith.

You're stuck, tied to the bone, imagine soar!

Gawking at the transparent entrée, hoping it's a miraculous elevator,

That will lift you above any earthly floor.

Or at least release you through the other side, the greener side.

Wondering why the solution didn't show up yet,

You're ready, the scheme is visible, and all is set;

To enter and hoard all in Sesame's store.

The key that's hidden behind your own reflection—

But to hold its essence creates a struggle and a tension.

You can see, but you can't touch,

Hope the back cast won't give you a bore!

Must know oneself and all else will follow!

The convoluted ease of the formula!

I know myself, you wonder, but what's that key?

That will permit me with angels to love and wallow?

Do I need a password to walk in and skip around?

And enjoy its Eden till morning's mist?

But what to do if they won't let me in?

Oh, my calm savage within!

Poor you are if you must

Hit the roof and punch your fist!

But, that's not my style!

Must charmingly win souls with a smile!

But stupid they're not, they know my gist.

So you question their reasonable plan,

Telling yourself, "I know I can!

But how could such a minimalism block my entrance?

Challenging my dimensions, and all what's more!"

The key that hides and protects itself so that you don't lead yourself astray,

By trying it on the wrong doors—It's a celestial key, not an earthly shore!

Size doesn't matter after all—a small key, but yes, I see!

So you keep up the search, you ask the doctor and the church.

But "Keep out of the reach of children," the notice reads!

Must grow now, you're here to lead.

Respect, bravery, and willpower are musts;

But not enough, must also be pure, not just tough.

To the faithful obstinate one fate will dine,

With stars, faith, and a few dreams,

Where the sky has no ceiling,

And of its miracles it's unveiling,

Admitted to that amazing feeling,

Which of your divinity is revealing,

Enfolded by flawless spirits—

But first meditate in peace; do your kneeling—

Can you imagine?! The key is in your dreaming!

So allow the stars to rain upon you,

As there's a thousand wishes to be made,

But first must end that inner war—

Stop concealing!

So if I understand well, Doorkeeper,

If I am to pass to the blessed side, I can't hide!

So if I ask you in confidentiality,

A few confessional questions in spontaneity,

Will you listen and not judge me?

As my ego has often lied!

So "all for one and one for all" is the key's test?

But how do I transform?! How do I have to be?!

How do I know what's best?

Can I become selfless? As a monkey is never a tree!

I can evolve, but I remain only me!

As I love myself, what's the harm in that?

A sure devotion and sincere passion—

And to the public, I can wear a different hat.

I must fly high, and reach my crest.

Carrying their burden crushes my chest.

I can't breathe, imagine nest!

Just leave me alone! Away from the cattle, away from the rest!

I'll make you money, just make your bet! Just invest!

And once in a blue moon, you're welcome for a day, be my guest.

Just come with a high spirit, not depressed.

And please! I love beauty, be well dressed.

Oh, Epiphany! Here you are!

My mind from perfection is clearly far!

It's evident now why I have no key;

I'm out of the way from Celeste.

Thank you, doorkeeper, now I understand;

I need more time to decipher my quest.

Annexe 4: Leeloo go! I need the secret of the key.

"God doesn't give anyone anything they can't handle!"

Just a statement to comfort sorrows!

Or that delay of fortune, love, or joy.

As we hold our breath for a better tomorrow.

Does the key remain hidden

For those who do not face their insightful essence?

Nor allow their consciousness to radiate with its supremacy!

Or feel its glorious presence!

Crisscrossing the maze only to reach ends,

Blinding themselves from the veiled pass—

Fearing to understand what it's for!

"Too much beyond me," they whisper to themselves,

"Why examine my spirit when I can score?!"

They don't try to see the silver lining,

And to their truth they are binding.

Always seduced by ephemeral desires,

In their contradictions and inner fires,

Consuming themselves is how they feed,

Then they wonder why they bleed!

Someday, they'll rise above themselves,

And face their pains and fears,

Then dare to open their hearts and ears

To the miracle in them and the world around them;

Only then, the revelation will be granted—in time—

For the ones who dared to explore.

Those who were not afraid to enter the gates of death

And be in ultimate union with their inner shrine.

Those who dream to be reborn in the fortified holy towns,

Which allow no ingress of evil or its roar.

Where existence pillars are the eternal reason of the spiritual,

Not the instinctive violence, that primitive ritual.

Annexe 5: Simplify please!

Keep on removing the resistance,

Relax and trust, stubbornly go your distance.

Let bad models leave you, positive be, and stay you.

Laugh with life, and it'll be in your assistance.

Perseverance, fiery waters, yes, that insistence.

Blossoming happens in its season to share its coexistence.

Centered and grounded be, it'll help your subsistence.

Take your time, and choose what's well,

As impulsive conquerors soon do lose,

And they fast check back in their hell.

The key is in a kindred spirit, and in peace of mind.

And a serene clear conscience is an ecstatic ride.

I hope I answered to what you need!

Just believe in your path, trust your story,

You're writing your future, not a screed!

I dreamt of an angel that gave me answers.

What enrichment! A spirit enhancer!

But must wake up now, I have to travel,

And be on my way for my mystery to unravel.

Annexe 6: What's in and what's out now!

"What exactly are you after?"

Last question of the doorkeeper for the day!

"I'm hunting for my most constant, loyal companions—

Inner light and peace," I respond;

"But I do not know how to get to their destination!

I'm hoping you will let me through,

So I can search and reach for it!" I plead.

But his solid face is enjoying the derision of me,

Staring at my fervid eyes with a calm dexterity of a clown.

Rolling the key through his fingers, and theatrically he says:

"Giving a child a sword to protect himself is silly.

Better teach him how to master himself through it.

Till he evolves to become the spiritual dilly! Before then,

The weapon might detach the heads he's trying to protect,

And the detachment here is far from non-material!

The child screams to his mother—interrupting her tea:

"Mother, hand me the sword; I can handle the game."

So you all scream to God, as children for the key."

"Very nice, mister, but can I see the boss, please?"

I must speak to Sesame,

He who holds the cryptic, not just display and tease!

Oh, Sesame, open—open to me,

Show me what destiny holds in store!

Then give me the code to the esoteric pass,

So I keep away from the obnoxious bore.

I need to be alone, and clear from the mass,

To understand what it's all about! And what's my life for?!

Doing the right thing was never my domain,

But I'm purging my soul now with heavenly rain.

I think I'm a light warrior, and that is my truth!

So now work your magic,

And give me a key from that mystical booth.

His answer was in the stillness sound,

In that dreary, contemptuous familiarity

Of that still movement, and vague transportation . . .

Thinking: "Hurry up, I'm going to miss my death!"

Running for something that isn't even there!

Speeding away, I just can catch my wonted breath.

The doorkeeper won't let me pass.

I'm stopped at the door.

It wasn't my time to see the joyous light.

The sweet death must wait. Mustn't it?!

Chapter 5

The Undertaker

I see a black shadow now; it's standing behind the doorkeeper!

It's growing taller and larger by the second.

It's approaching in this dark alley, covering my light, capturing my rage!

How can I make the shadow of fear, fear my awesome might?!

Perhaps by riding on a mystical glance faster than my mind's dance!

In a car driven by wild black horses that will fly me out of this limbo;

As I watch their charcoal manes race against the wind.

Swept away I am, into oblivion, and away from my danger.

He'll forget me, and find someone else to chase.

But run again?! No! I promised myself to stand and wait!

Maybe, he is a friend, after all!

Or simply an accomplice to my end!

He might lead me to my way! Is he my heavenly guide?!

Oh, I see him clearly now, a loyal friend, indeed!

Will stay with me after the last gulp of air,

That final out cold encounter! I'll say hello, but I'm now blind.

How am I supposed to find my heaven now?

Oh, I can still see, but not further than my nose!

Facing this most charming souvenir—what a lethal package!

A coffin! He knows how to pack a breathtaking gift!

This is too much, must cool down, hand me a beer!

I'll shake my head to clear this horrid vision,

But senseless I feel in this misprision!

It's a curious world. I was close, but, not enough!

A free pass, but to the wrong flight!

The soul of death is here for me.

To hold me once, and never more! How humbling!

I was dreaming of the idyllic light,

Now gravity is pulling me to the perishable sight!

Eternity isn't for mortals, I know!

And why would I want to live further?!

For another slander, another animosity, and another murder!

My mind made sense when I took on the fight.

Am I now rambling?

A falling angel! Calling myself for comfort!

Feels better than witnessing my present status,

As an evil sent home! Oh, no! I was lost but happy to roam!

Immortality is out of reach—is that what we should teach?!

You'll perish and die—is that the message?! Worth the effort!

Who said that is my truth?!

Goddamn it! I'm rather moral, and still in my youth!

Oh, mercy, dear Lord!

"Please send me an angel, and let her wings unfold.

You're a clement God! That's what I've been told!

I thought finally someone cared, revealed to me were You.

Do I blaspheme if I ask; did You lie to me too?!

And if there is someone out there to protect my soul,

Will you show me who?!

God, if you talk back sometimes, maybe now is good.

Schizophrenic I'm not, but I'm in a deadly hood!

Where it's believed that the road to heaven is through hell!

Am I being taken there dressed in a wooden overcoat?

Positive I am, but this is not very well!

Shall I fight or flight? Show me what's right!"

I thought I would be a manifestation of your miracles,

The chance of new beginnings, new balanced love, becoming the oracle.

To heal the children, and lead them to sincerity, and integrity!

Wasn't it all about the above? Overcoming the test of the obstacle!

Snap out of it, now, I order myself.

Disband these obsessions. This can't be!

It's just a delusion for that burdened guilt I carry,

As errors, I've made many.

I dared what they call hopeless and faced my fears,

While I led, they sat in the rear.

I dared to love and to lose—those sins I had to choose.

I could never have known otherwise,

If I sat desperate, and crunched the dice!

Now for my experience I must pay!

Could the price be my own decay?!

As umbrage is hunting me, and not just today!

Must be my imagination!

I'll take another exit, and be on my way."

But fearful, I think,

In my series of mirrors still so many shadows to defeat.

Oh, that intricate web— never a bright evident way out!

Will I have the strength to resolve all this yet still be on my feet?

What a strange feeling!

That I'll be trapped in every egress till I face what I'm running from.

If I just knew what it is exactly!

Could it be the price-tag on my purifying dress?

I know it's my conscience that awoke,

Or simply my backstabbing remorse that provokes,

Convincing me that joy I do not deserve,

And I might as well lose my vim and verve.

But enough with this nonsense, enough with this talk—

I shall take things in hand and my chastisement revoke.

As I am not falling that easily, mortality boy!

I will fight back with a will of Troy.

I won't lay and play dead,

You must combat if you want my head.

Swift, this will not be—

To steal from me this hard-earned key.

I do not dread you, fear is easy,

I shall fight with dignity, no, not this!

I'm ready for you, come out now.

I know how to contend with a black shadow.

Yes, I must know how.

But still movement! Vague transportation!

I shall know all in its time, if I have time.

Meanwhile, seeking heaven on earth is such a persecuting torture.

But my persistent spirit is determined to understand.

The puzzle of the maze is at present bigger than my human complexity.

But in certainty I stand, knowing that God will save the day.

Too much left to do, it can't be my time! Not just yet.

The much greater person in me is still incognito— clearly, also to myself!

Chapter 6

Cruel That Paradise

Annexe 1: Where is that stop?!

8th of March 2007

I flew back to a coma reality; that I certainly had a visa for.

Where the steady ambiguous dominates, standing blindly at that crossroads,

Shifting my head as a marionette right and left;

My stare with its lid broadly shut,

Yet, hoping my Master will sign me the green light.

Kneeling dependently in the midst of passage,

Sleepwalking hoping for a better trance;

With that stale taste which invades deeply my throat,

Howling, growling an inaudible roar,

To calm my savage spirit that seldom longs to be tamed—

That inner rebellion that gives me the persistence to walk the extra mile.

That reputation of madness which licences my freedom to test existence!

Life's high and low! No trouble at all, I can handle.

But that nature of mankind, for any sign of weakness,

A thousand volunteers, on your veins, ready to stab their blades,

To contemplate on your gladiatorial resistance!

Witness how you wade, and if you fade!

It was good to challenge, distract, and entertain.

Call it a sacrifice for the higher good!

Always give the plebs a reason to feel better!

Why not comfort their limits?

Their favourite scene, show a master on his knees.

Around the fiery pot, they dance the yum-yum,

Barking; we will eat tonight. "*Houga souga nouga fouga!*"

Annexe 2: Why is their heaven my hell?

What most find entertaining, I do fear,

Annoys and bores me.

Their asinine aspersions simply stupefy me.

In their presence, I must while away the time,

While they wish that I justify me!

Most of them are to me as noise.

I can't wait for it to sleep,

So I can have my saintly poise!

Meanwhile, the utopian wonder upon the words of winds

And hear the rose sing a good morning to earth!

While it salutes the meadows and the moths,

Waiting to emerge with a miracle's birth!

As angels swing their legs on giant trees,

To manifest divine miracles to sanctify me!

Be that as it may, there are bills to be paid, I understand!

And children to be cared for and their demands are as raids!

It's just a privilege to observe and edify! So much at hand!

Must survive or conquer, win, and impress!

But the world you witness is the one you make!

Your inner riches must you fake?

Sleeping under the starry skies!

That high! Is just for a vacation!

And if you can swim in deep litany,

Who wants to wake!

Today you must indulge upon wars,

And respect its time duration!

In a sick world fed by greed and blood,

By the innocent used as flesh to serve!

Knowing that keeps me alone!

My peace of mind, I'll never trade.

Maybe someday, I'll share my heart! But now,

Time for my soul, I must reserve.

As I give them love, and they give me war,

Maybe it's my expectation's mistake!

In faith, I introduce them to my loved ones and flora life.

But trusting them is like trusting a cannibal dinner to make!

Among them heaven seems as an endless lie!

I see their world as a masquerade.

Where you're always welcome to join in,

On a red carpet where the devil grins,

"Look who's here! Oh, well, well, well!

Annexe 3: Be pragmatic, they counsel!

A world with two moons,

In a dream, I roamed there.

I saw its evolution, culture, and civilisation,

Where dignities are preserved, and nothing is bare.

A delusion that you may call harmless, if you care!

As testing why God is radiant! Could it be that crème sample?

Which made him look so brilliant and fair?

But some cattle are too spiteful and to harm they dare.

Tonight, we offer a pure soul to the serpent, for example!

So illusions may manifest!

Dark spirits party! Is not a plaything, my boy!

So watch out when you think you're being coy,

Everything has its price!

The return of your evil—you'll pay thrice.

When the wicked boomerang you threw is back in your face to destroy.

It's an iniquitous fare to pretend you're fate-master;

Careful! With that you shouldn't toy!

Out of my mind! Indeed I am.

Why try to simulate rational in an irrational world?

Where all play "life," in a world dominated by controlled folly

And un-cathartic ambition! When their egos are threatened,

They batter you as if the act is natural tradition.

("Be pragmatic, be realistic!" *The lemming's counsel,*

We are limited, be content,

Walk soulless, just do the thing—

Money, profit—our way! You know!

Poetry is for dreamers; shouldn't dream.

Dreams are for sleepers. Just be like us, get real!

Just follow the trend.

Don't you try our rules to bend!

Hear our silence—it's so sad!

"Still" desolation is nobler than mad.

The happy ending is just for movies.

The world's painful truths we can't mend;

And authenticity is not so groovy!

Just let us blabber together in empty levity.

Sex in oblivion! Why not?!

As in a fearful humming calm,

Misery always appreciates any simulated beauty.

Yes, true wealth is within!

We just have to cut ourselves open, and grab it.

No wonder there are so many bloodbaths,

And too many bleeding souls cause red seas—

A horizon of exploded paint of fiery waters,

A lovely sight for a verse!

Still, upon God's design, let us not "fairly" curse!)

One mile at a time my mind,

Awaiting my new divinely ordered fate, I think,

Above and beyond—blue waters are much more celestial than red!

Easier concept to accept, without a hesitant blink!

No need for bloodshed over expressions written in ink . . .

Annexe 4: Fall as a puppet to the ground!

Can we become humbler and kinder as a race?

Can I?! Will I?!

As death comes to us as an inner thief and snaps the soul!

Suddenly, we fall in a moment of prime, as a garment to the ground;

Robbed of a dignified goodbye!

With astonished eyes pervaded with the one question?

Did I deserve to live or die?

Annexe 3: Wings upon my curving shoulders

07th July 2007

I was an alien in no man's land.

While each entity signs its name upon the air it breathes.

I have no inner abode, no home, and no shelter,

Wishing the skies to adopt me,

And give birth to my most exquisite clandestine desire—

To be converted into an angel and discover my wings,

Those upon my curving shoulders,

Forcing, ripping their way through my human skin.

Knowing that the labour of a new life is arduous,

Still longed for it in the origin of the night.

Flouting the ravenous scathing beauty thieves,

Those life-inhalers with vultures' eyes,

Waiting to audition the ins and outs.

Standing by to attack,

Plunder, and devour any chaste moral or drive.

While sneering, leering lasciviously at its naive unattended prey,

"Aaouuu, Aaouuu! Do not fret! I'm your Frey.

Annexe 4: Hello, Phoenix

13th of October 2007

For miracles, I yearned in my simple soul—

That a great spirit will love, guide, and comfort me.

But ironically, an expedient phoenix appears,

With his peculiar, prickly wings that glitters.

Facing me with a shadowy smirk, and open fiery arms, ready for the embrace!

I knew then, it wasn't the rescue in my darkest hour, but precisely that hour.

Amid a cyclone of dust, he emerges to devour me with questions.

Can't help wondering if it is his dust or mine!

Was it the sky that is on fire or was it I?

Blazing flames in the reflection of my blinkered astounded eyes;

My vision started to blur, my psyche drifts to slightness.

My mind was the engine of thoughts, suddenly I went mute.

Standing still in stillness, Him and I,

Observing, glaring at the moment with psyches wide open

As that incessant night flips me an image of my sinister half,

It seems clearer now that his rays are not my dawn.

Chapter 7

Golden Fields

Annexe 1: The black rose!

The instant of my crucial test of faith is upon me,

And finally the gate is broadly ajar, but as if for a dreadfully singular service.

That's the doorkeeper standing in the black suit,

With a long black coat, in the closing shades of that windy night.

Behind the gate, the wheat fields I always saw in my dreams—

Oh, those dreams were such a reliable escape!

But what seduces me by and large, ends up with quiet a soul's rape!

He is not holding me back anymore, but stretching his hand,

Inviting me to take a black violet rose—

Attractive as the tango sadness, I approach.

121

His sight on my meaning,

A chill that froze my vanity in time!

Yet it's a white, summery dress I'm wearing.

My hands are empty, my face is pure.

My eyes are glaring, my heart is daring.

Light to the light I go, with my hopes and genuine intentions.

If expatriated from encumbrance, I accept the detention.

Over with that fight, let it be morning, enough with the night.

Signs are talking, on track at last.

I'm ready for the trip, did cast away the past.

Fate is favouring me, angels joined me, and it wasn't fast.

Or it isn't over yet!

After all my insane daring, and all I put on the line?!

After all my cosmic bet!

With sharks, I dove in the deepest waters,

So why am I received by the fiery porter?!

I took the chance to rid my arrogance from its rights,

And all I claimed to be a green sign!

I must stop paying for my life's show a fine after fine!

I teleported to the divine,

Took a train to reach what's mine.

I walked, I drove—what's left?

A ship! Or, maybe, I can afford a private jet!

I threw my last chip with my last smile.

Leave me now, no more challenges in a slough!

If I may, I'll skip the hero's call,

Here's another number to dial.

But it seems that I must stand the final trial.

The doorkeeper is addressing me again, voicelessly!

Or is he interrogating?

Would you make the same choices knowing what you know now?

Are you ready to liberate your regressive forces and the material world?

Under the irresistible temptation would you still yield?

That startling, unspoken sound mesmerises me no more.

Yet overwhelms my consciousness of whomever I once knew as I.

I keep pushing my feet to a place they don't necessarily care or dare to face,

But they must resist the need to succumb, to collapse.

No one will carry me to my mortal bed, my grave.

Or maybe my loyal new friend, the undertaker, was real after all!

Annexe 2: A stranger in a strange land!

Hello, my trendy monstre du jour"!

You're sent to me to find golden fields—

And I haven't anything to give.

No panic there, in my spring, I'll be healed.

As I have a million triumphs to live.

But he sees me bare, believing I'm a dead stick.

I can't reverse my seasons from "tac" to tic!

In this most arid land, even an *Olivier* can't bear an olive!

Just come on, shadowy creature, and give me my peace!

Haul what you claim as yours.

As I must know by now, I'll rest when I give up the ghost.

Me in confusion playing brave,

Not decoding if my imminent end is a welcoming friend, or abrasive foe.

Whatever it may be, every willing step carries me towards the exit,

That will lead me out of my tormented being, and my burdened ways of
life!

*Heavenly Mother! I admit my defeat to you with a
song!*

But first, do you hear me humming for help? For rescue!

My spirit is frayed, and need audacity dew!

And it's inevitably nourished by the sight of you!

As I feel shorthanded and in a constant struggle,

Yet I'm humble in trouble. So, I must renew!

I'm really withered here, with a smile upon my face,

Penniless, homeless, friendless, and my head in space,

Witnessing leisurely the humanly disgrace!

Still hoping with your miracles, joy I'll embrace.

Divine Father,

I know that you don't take pride in my fall!

And I can swear that you heard my call.

I also know that there's no shield from this rest,

As the shadow of death hunts its own angel, if he knows its best.

I surrender to my fate,

But this is not the way I envisaged supremacy of premises!

A coffin and no one to carry it!

A stranger in a strange land!

Holding a black rose! Not like this! Not just yet!

Damn it! Don't let me die now!

I'm way away from my perfection.

At least, I die trying to live. Live better.

That nostalgia that "aches" me for a world I enjoyed once,

In half-remembered life, in another space and time!

The traces of memories, laughter, and beings I loved.

Or was that also a contender-dream?

I've been told that the darkest hours are just before the dawn,

It is charcoal black in here—where is that light?!

I cross that gateway now fearing it's a dead end.

In my last rush, thinking:

Am I lost in a narrow one-way street?

Or am I just rejecting the ending scene?

Did I waste my life in vain?

In my fraught rush to depart,

Have I taken the wrong train?!

"Faute de mieux," I hope that my burnt ashes

Will purge and prepare my new grounds.

As phoenix became my friend, we've met many times.

He'll carry my dust again,

And tempest in meandering tornado into the skies,

Where angels prepared my evolution ceremony

With love, where there's no disdain.

I'll rest if I must; yes, I'll lie in this coffin;

Just please write for my loved ones my new address;

Write upon it my name.

Annexe 3: My funeral's song

15th of July 2007

Titled: It's my coffin you're carrying!

It's my coffin you're carrying! Oh, dear God, I'm dead!

Please! Carry it to glory, let me rise with a straight head.

Hand me a candle in the dark, just to see the last shadow I shed.

I am knocking; open up! Can't you feel?! I have a heart to mend!

Oh, wait! I'm seeing the light from above! Oh, lord, I am in the red!

I heard a voice say, "Surrender." That couldn't be any tender!

"Let go, daughter. I am not here to slaughter!

It's time for you to go. Where?! For me to know."

In my silence, and fear I tried, to whisper my last breath and said:

"I wish I were sweeter and kinder, and in my manners much, much milder.

In my love, a passionate finder, in my heart, I shout louder,

In my dreams, a wild hunter, and in my faith, a belief that's blinder.

But now it's too late; I lie helpless in my mortal bed."

Then I awoke, from another world that provoked,

I opened my eyes and understood, I'd been given another chance

To mend my errors and ways, to a higher dream I rose to play,

With a new breath of life, a blissful path I chose to pipe / to light

Annexe 3: The realization of my ignorance!

What a lugubrious provoking dream!

Quite a revealing song!

I wake up now shattered yet keen;

I have a new chance to cast my wrong.

Life is clement and will forgive me:

For the hearts and promises I broke,

To drive away my upheaval!

For intimidating others by playing the strong,

For my grandeur's retrieval!

For having the malicious invoked,

To protect me from a higher evil!

For putting people on the wrong track,

So when they stab, it won't be in my back.

For chasing change and remaining the strange,

To decipher all in my mind's cage.

But some of my sins, I learned from you, my Lord!

As leaving my door wide open to see how they dash and conquer!

And giving them free will to test how much they'll abuse.

Gifting them grandeur's illusion to discover how they'll treat the meek!

As the faster I see through them, the faster I can discard them.

Isn't that human! But what about you, my Lord!

Is that why You love your solitude?

Did they disappoint you too?

Once after once, and once more!

Heavenly father! I need to come to you, now!

I'll cleanse my spirit and resurrect!

With this pure new heart, nothing to correct!

I'm ready. Cherubs are here,

Wrapping me in an infant suede sheets!

How wonderful! What an angelic treat!

To fly me to heavens and win it all!

Wait a minute! This cover is labeled:

"Made of your skin, 100% purged hide!"

Claustrophobia is playing its tricks on me!

Stop now! I'm so beat!

But didn't the fear help me stay free?

And my paranoia that kept me safer!

Or was it only my serenity's waiver?

I keep walking escaping my every feeling!

A fleeing heart! Yes, of me unveiling!

I'm fenced in by edges on all fronts,

And my wings are still buried under my curving shoulders,

As I go away with the fairies…!

But, earth seems to be calling…!

I realize now that I must stop in the midst of my deserts,

This road is infinite; I'm not equipped to run forever!

I swallow my breath, and with a silent gasp, I dare to turn,

As I look behind me, to my maddest surprise, I find no one there!

No one is following me! I'm all alone! All these years I ran from monsters!

But there is not even a shadow! I laughed in hysteria for all the years I ran,

Then I kneeled on my lands of sand, and wept!

All what I created were ghosts! Maybe just to keep me company!

It's time for my healing! I will kiss the loving new tomorrow.

At present, nothing to me is more welcome.

Annexe 4: I would like to go now! I want peace.

Another day, another dream, another morning!

The morning, I love; filled with promises, and hope.

But now, I think it is the time to sleep!

I close my eyes, but the voice is back, the voice is here!

Oh, this daily nightmare is talking, all over again!

Am I still in my purgatory?! Why isn't this all over yet?!

And if my ghosts were only ghosts, why won't they shut up?

Why won't I let them go? Do I dread boredom more than monsters?

Why do I let them pour poison in my diamond cups?

Just to entertain the dull reality of things!

Or maybe because I lead them to believe that they can!

So I can penetrate in their true ghastly intentions!

It saves me time and effort just to let them be!

Then let them go without regrets!

I was always accused of doubting too much. But here,

I give them the benefit of the doubt. And the more I give it,

The more I know it's all what I'm left with.

Presently, this is the least of my burden,

As I'm accompanied by the faint echo of my unsound poise!

Silence voice, silence!

Even in my stillness there is so much noise!

Let's make a pact, or raise the stakes!

Here what I propose, it may be worth you the deal!

Let me go in peace, and don't interrupt my death.

You'll have some sensitivity, and you'll leave me alone!

As you can see, I'm taking the depth.

You'll let me hear that stillness sound,

And let the calm prevail! Now, hush! Hush!

While I release my last breath, you must leave me with my roots!

I'm going under, under the mysterious grounds.

In return, I let you care to sing a song of love!

While the ocean rides another wave!

Who needs to yearn when in heavens above!

There, I'll take you on rendezvous, why not then to the paradise bay?

Where you don't need to hide your trace! Or stand guard upon a grave!

Or bury your conscience with lace gloves, while fearing to perish and decay!

We can rise to be higher spirits! So we were fools, and who weren't?

All our weaknesses we can beat, and achieve the divine union's perfection!

Ah, with this snigger I may be told that wining in heaven is for hell a defeat!

The voice won't let me sleep.

Seducing me to writhe and turn!

How am I going to get through this frozen night?

I can light a fire to burn my cowards in their hell!

But I can't get warmed by that!

I will hear them shout! Fearing the flames and its light!

No, voice! Your misery, I won't reap.

I'll stay awake, in faith, for my "raison d'être" to be revealed!

My serenity, harmony and peace, I'll reach.

But I'm harassed in my own skin,

And what is this amplified repulsed uproar for?! A reminder maybe!

To pacify myself about being different! Crazy, strange, special,

There isn't an insane name that I haven't been called.

Maybe I just miss my heavens while walking with the vain cattle!

I'll find my reasons, just shut up!

What I need now is divine guidance!

Here you are my angel, and I hear you say:

"You are good, and you know it.

Embrace life, my girl, you took the leap!

And if every sadness reveals new insights,

You are indeed among the wise.

Stronger angel you became,

You chose the battles worth the fight!

You dared the ridicule and held the grin,

And, that my girl is a master's guise.

You carried your pain as an earth its mountains,

And waited in faith for your voice to rise!

It's not your "Karma" that caused your sorrow,

But the hate and judgment in their eyes!

We'll heal you now so you can heal them.

Then we'll fly you soon through the starry skies,

Your soul is pure; now gain your wings,

As one angel's kiss, is worth an eternity, as a mighty king!

You are among us; just follow your bliss, and heart's advice.

Did that mean that I no longer climb alone?

And through that door, I'm authorized?!

Shall I deem that as a whisper or another dream?

I'll remain calm and patient, my reason, I must keep.

I'll survive this, I trust. I just must.

Till I meet the excellence that lies ahead.

My heart promised me a heavenly breeze,

And I undoubtedly believe it.

Chapter 8

Intrepid Spirit Warrior is Facing the Soul of Death!

Intrepid inner warrior, please! Abandon me not now!

The angel of death is behind my shield, knocking, snarling,

Enjoying his upper hand with his playful caress, feeling,

Sniffing my shadow, and my waning innate scent,

Breathing frostily behind my ear, murmuring:

"Boo, boo! Did I scare you?!

Don't you frown, my child; at least not yet.

I am not here to hurt, or you to threaten.

But to grant you another chance, only if your own soul you enhance,

Before your ashes turn to dust, you will learn what you must.

Understand that the dark force which you call your towers

Is just wind, and not the sun that empowers.

The poisonous anger that you hold, is the prison bars of your mould.

Holding back your mystery to unfold, stagnating your being for some gold!

Promise to live, and from your heart to give,

To have compassion, and to harness your passion.

Kind be and respect the line, with yourself and also thine!

Don't be eager to ostensibly shine, discretion is particularly fine.

Moderate your fiery temper, towards what you call mediocre, and a whimper.

Meditate on life, God, and angels, in stillness you will find your marvels.

Allow others their way to see, how their life best should be.

Tolerate the differences my daughter, to live, and let live without slaughter.

Then your suffering will cease, when in humility you stand and in peace."

The ultimo ultimatum is negotiating my life and soul with me—

A frightening honour! I'm staunch yet with a trembling soul I utter:

"Maybe I'm at the end of my strength and wit, but my soul is not for the bet.

I promise to change my unconsecrated ways as 180 turns to zero.

But before I accolade the honours of the salvation hero,

Can I retreat to better understand?

How accurately my intrinsic values stand! And if they stand!

In the face of mediocre ways---

That mass production of androids sewn in sombre days!

Will I be granted the bravery for a vastness of spirit—

To become holy, mighty kind, and inspirit!

He stares deeply into my soul, then steps back and whispers:

"*Carpe Diem*, my girl.

 Go in fortune, go in peace.

I'll be watching you, don't be fierce.

Retreat, my daughter, if you must,

But careful after what you lust.

In between and here and there,

I'll protect you till you return."

"Return where?!" I think!

But I bow to his grace, and speak:

"In gratitude I thank you, my "nobler" steer,

For the granted time to tempt and learn.

How to deal with mediocrity when we've dined with Gods?!

And thrown in dungeons in morose nights to reside!

And being repelled and criticized by inane ogres for that dream—

Because where I reside, all is spurious, everything is surely how it seems—

I'll question myself till I find the answer,

Till I reach that grace of the heavenly dancer.

I just hope while dancing with mortals,

That I do not forget the eloquent moves of the "dance".

Chapter 9

Stillness Sound

27th of January 2007

What's that stillness?! What's that sound?

Is it silence?! That drives me to numbness, with no ground?

What's that game?! Is it my mind? Going insane?!

What's that question?! Who am I?!

That old refrain—In vain, in vain.

Am I alone? Is God with me?

Or am I just a hopeful dreamer

Trying to camouflage Her pain?

Do I have a destination? Or do I only strut with empty time?

Entombed in my own womb, for a meaningful reason to entwine!

Is the world lost in its complexity? Or is it I?

In my contradictions, I shan't deny.

I can no longer run from myself.

My thoughts chase me as predators,

And I am the victim of my own wonders,

Pretending life is not a theatre; staged before a karmic mirror.

Didn't I promise myself the world? I ask myself, my lord!

But bury those thoughts of worlds!

Why pursue? Why figure?

Shall I continue the quest for the secrets of life?

When the hunt is lethal, why not let go?! Why track the strife?!

And why on my own skin, I test the knife?

I say, hold a minute! Did my torture, I begin it?

I shake every second, turning each moment upside down.

Awaiting you near, God! Will You just beckon?!

In that silent silence, where nothing moves!

I'm embalmed in reluctance, where nothing breathes.

Too big for me, those assumptions!

Would I have to be mad to continue? To delve deeper!

Didn't You, God, advise "dying to life," the alter ego?

Me and me! See and see!

Can I instead just die for a while from the outer self?

If the earthly choices impose to be!

Yes, I die every day, from my twisted old ways,

Trying to evade the curtains of darkness from veiling the eye of my soul;

Forcing myself to stand tall! Survival, isn't it all?!

The devil whispers "Join us." What a ball!

Banality seductively calls; no longer my call.

I chose a psychic death, on a cold day.

Desperately climbing the mystic ladder, in an obscure cloud,

To reach God's station. Where is that stop?!

"Leap empty-handed into the void, do not fear!" A shout in my ear.

"Will you dare that leap of faith?!

Are you worthy of your gifts?!

Will you search your own heart to find its aim?!

Will you eventually catch the evolutionary train?!"

I scream inaudibly with a straight face,

"Yes, yes!" In my mind of minds, I know I can, I am, I will.

I now soar, pondering on my invisible wings,

And the marvelous world beneath me that seem so small!

A fright invades my wings, oh, this divine height!

As I wonder, did I deserve this angelic flight? In shielded doubt, I fall!

I descend, in sadness, fear, and awe to face my gruesome death.

I let go now, I never knew how to fly! Now, I know why.

Everyone witnessed my fall, but what they didn't know was

That the hour of the Lazarus wolf summoned my noble resurrection,

My own, my life.

In my compelling patience, could that stillness voice be?

The sound of the quantum forces in me!

The silence between the notes, composing the meaning,

The melody of my essence!

The same majestic roots that created a tree!

I was salvaged by a white cloud, no longer black.

The same cloud that with its face of desolation took me down,

Now, raises, breaths, reconstructs and saves me.

One mysterious day the darkness must dispel,

The glowing rays are apt for summoning.

They must illuminate and radiate through me,

To be the light herder, only the shepherd tolerates and waits.

Patience, my soul, patience!

You need time to harvest yourself.

So much left to understand,

Yes, I'm in my time. I'm on my way.

Chapter 10

Awoke in a Humble Grace

I realize years later through all this,

And talk about slow understanding!

To harmonize my soul, don't need to win a volatile game,

Nor have to be the rebel standing.

Yet I'll keep searching for a higher consciousness,

And for what is pure and true.

Till I find the ultimate answer. Damn it, it is so due!

Sincere I became, but I still catch my lips stumbling upon a lie;

Genuine I stay, but sometimes the truth I still deny.

I ran from my fate one too many times,

Till I faced my heart, through these abstruse rhymes.

Now, I know my call and I understand why.

To misery, it's time to say enough. Go! Bye-bye.

My faith is as unshakable as my dreams;

I trust my venture and follow my stream.

And in a humble grace I kneel,

For the gratitude I do feel!

I walk in pride, and shout my mind under the bliss of rain.

Now I know what remains.

Crazy, I've been called,

When I put my life on hold

Nobody understood my lord,

The mysteries yet to unfold!

The superficiality of the social function,

Defines my resurrection by my sales!

For them, a star is in a camera's flash,

And feeling whole is in the cash;

And that, my dear, is no tale.

How is your book selling, is the main question!

That's what they call a heavenly junction.

Denying that the miraculous abundance is in the dream!

The divine within is not in trying to seem!

It is not in Gucci and Dior, where you will find your cure.

The cure is in your silence and your tears.

The cure is in your patience, face your fears.

The cure is in your prayers and your faith,

It is in your compassion and ideal passion.

The cure is in your humble kneeling,

The sweet vengeance is in forgiveness,

That's the way to a truthful healing.

In my quest for happiness, I found my light,

It was before my eyes, behind my sight.

I'll hold my ground and enjoy the exploration,

The minds I must meet and their divine cooperation,

In deciphering and healing this life's story,

Fulfilling my divine within is my greatest glory!

Getting to enlightenment is never simple.

It takes ages to build a temple.

One mile at a time my mind; maybe on my next exploration

I'll take a revolutionary car—

To know if we can change in essence, or if we are just what we are.

In this journey, I walked alone,

With an angel or a few!

Then faced my call, stared at my fate,

To know that thing I was born to do!

I took the leap of the unknown,

And how exhilarating was the view!

I tested myself to the very core,

And why I was so terribly blue.

Angels collecting wishes from the stars are always there,

If I just had that clue!

I would have had patience for my dreams,

For my treasures, and all what's true.

In serenity, I nurtured my magic,

While most fostered their vicious zoo!

Who would have shown me that my love was within?

And here's the answer that was due.

I prayed soulfully to be so rich and free,

While having been all along! Realizing it was all I had to do.

How I waited for the blessings of this calm certainty!

Oh, the manifestations of the promised new!

Chapter 11

No True Victory Without a Noble Destination

When darkness was all around me,

Mindlessly, I pondered why!

I was in my own womb, forming my inner tie,

Wondering why life had forsaken me—

Why that deny?!

I'd forgotten that the flower opens in its time,

And if rushed, it will wane and die.

Now in patience, I pray for my light!

And try to ignore my vanity's delights.

I create beauteous vibes and that's my home.

I expand, radiate, and there I roam.

I walk and live through my dreams.

I follow no one, and my rivers stream.

In my "minds", waterfalls I comb!

I believe in the best, yes, gastronome!

I sail through storms not dumbed with fear,

I challenge my absolutes, my far and near.

In happiness, I'll live, and right up to the end,

With my truest friend, and that was I.

Joy, I brought and received, truly not deceived!

I'll leave this earth with a glorious goodbye,

Not the one with one less scum!

And meet my heaven as a golden light,

While my angels sing: "What a glorious ray, O, welcome"!

Courage and bliss I wish you if you take this road,

As there will "heart-quakes" in most episodes.

So if you talk alone in your silence,

Know it's no madness.

And if you walk your way within trust,

It's far from artless!

Doubts will visit your rising soul,

And test your gigantic sadness,

While feeling naked and alone,

In your combat, poor and armless!

But do enlighten, your doorkeeper, and loudly whisper:

"I am here to quest and question.

I'm after my light, not my pension!

I'll stand the test; I'll bear the sway.

I wish for my best, I'll catch the ray.

I'll search the extraordinary in my human face,

While they live by their phone!

I'll bathe in the impossible, and welcome the unknown.

I'll travel the lengths to reach the depths of my soul.

I'll unmask my meaning, and my call.

I'll live my visions against all odds,

I deserve the good, I dared to fall."

That was my story, and it was no fiction,

To inspire, and release some tension;

To find your authentic self, it's not cash you need!

But out with your inner trash. Before it's too late!

You can't mend yourself after you became cinder and ash!

No easy way to break the cycle,

Must walk the line if you want the miracle!

Let go of your past, maybe give it a glance or two!

Keep advancing till around heavens you flew.

And when loneliness becomes the snuggling solitude,

You may your star pursue.

Call upon your adoring evolution that will set you free,

And wish for every plentitude.

Wander the universe upon your will,

Sure you deserve that altitude.

And once you felt that magnitude,

You'll long to live forever and a day!

And you'll celebrate your own existence,

For finding your sincere play!

That's your art that you'll share,

So you'll help those with an open heart.

Enjoy your new wish and its dream,

Believe in your vision, and its theme.

Then embrace yourself with loving light.

Oh, that reconciliation…!

As what is a victory without a noble destination!

Chapter 12

I Believe in the Incredible!

Oh, how gracious I feel, and can't say it was sudden!

The garden of light within me has blossomed, and I finally reckon,

That my dormant sources were always parts of heaven.

Now I witness this miraculous incredible bliss,

The world shines upon me with a constant heavenly kiss.

Thank you, my lord, for making me more you, for making me like this!

A few years of yesterdays, I was lost, not knowing what to do!

But my faith, patience, and hope I kept firm,

Praying daily to learn what I must learn.

I was claustrophobic and blue,

Wishing I mastered all what's true!

Serenity and clarity came as due,

With my soul challenging the new.

I now know, absolution is first from the self- asked,

Not in punishing ourselves, believing we're doing God's task.

And spotting the sadist for the bitter to swallow!

Forgive ourselves, we must; and nature will follow.

Life will forgive you, just ask!

In its beloved nobility to bask and wallow!

Let go now, and pray for what's good.

That's the life you should have, happy to be you should.

Don't say: Ah, only if I could!

All is possible, believe in the incredible;

You'll see the invisible, yes, you would.

Every morning, say to your inner king:

All is good in heavens, and all is good in my world.

Believe it, feel it, breathe it, let the light, light bring.

I am happy to share with you all this.

I am healed, as a miracle I feel, a miracle that is.

And God knows it's real, and you saw how,

Just when you connect to your goodness vow

Where you drift to the heavenly trance,

Where there's always a communication dance!

Sitting on his star that came from Mars,

Reached an angel holding my memoirs!

He put his soul upon my shoulder and said:

Surrender to happiness, my friend,

Today, put your misery to an end.

You were destined to send love and light.

Light is your destiny, just love song and light.

To this enchanted new beginning, I opened my soul.

All this heavenly order when only chaos I felt!

When I couldn't breathe,

Jammed and clustered by harrowing echoes;

Wondering if God was keeping score!

Suddenly, I hear my verses in my head spinning,

As a nostalgia, a remembrance! It felt like winning:

"*Carpe diem*, my girl,

Go in fortune, go in peace.

We'll be watching you, don't be fierce!

Retreat, my daughter, if you must,

But careful after what you lust!

In between and here and there,

We'll protect you till you return,

Return to us; that's where.

Living a breathtaking spiritual journey,

Demands faith and kindness, my dreamy child, and wonder!

And after the endurance, tolerance, and the bravery,

You'll recall your aim, in your marvelous ponder.

Knowing that your paradise, in its time, will unveil,

Just dare to emerge, and life will grow fonder.

Are you ready for your prime?

Wake up! Wake up!

Chapter 13

Let the Blood Flood Into Your Face!

What an adventure I lived! So esoterically intense!

If you're ready to live it, embrace its joys,

But not through the human sense!

Heaven is revealed to those who believe,

The secret is in your faith, makes perfect sense!

Trust in miracles, all will be good;

Self- destruction shall not intrude.

Start with yourself, that's a prelude!

Must feed your soul; that could be shrewd!

Do your part, from idiocy, stay apart.

Fight your daemon that's a start.

Search your light, heal your heart.

Find your way, spread the art.

Remember now, that's what:

The thing you were so sure of is not.

And the thing that you didn't see is the plot.

In wonder, you'll discover what you forgot.

Once your heart is open, you won't miss the shot.

Find your joy and dance with grace,

Dance life well, and let the blood flood into your face.

Share your bliss, with those who love your hug and kiss.

Intend to live your dream.

No matter how improbable it may seem.

Want what you want, even if a plane or a yacht.

Spirituality is abundance of all what's good,

Choose the ace, no guilt, if you want a lot.

Condition is, love your act and hurt no race.

But the question remains:

Who are you when you have not?

Are you enough to be without?

Search your soul till you are—

Then have it all, have it your way,

In both bays, in the" in" and the out!

So when you hear words of the hereafter, and here's a piece:

All is good in my world, and all is good in heavens! Snigger not in vain.

Have faith in the highest seven, as an innocent swain.

Vanquish the need others to please, please the inner you.

Enter the heavenly ease within, what a peaceful view!

You are loved by yourself, and that's the biggest love of all.

The exile fades, and your blood warms up, full house of spades!

Feeling complete is a rightful harmony. It's no caprice.

Light needs love and a sagacious mind.

Any vain cattle can scorn and shame.

Natural for a shark to tear out a piece!

And for a prey to hide its grain!

Nature is and will never cease;

But the genius is in finding the peace,

Even while any predator aims.

Don't persecute yourself, find your truth.

Crawling in darkness towards God's brain!

If you're addicted to pain, now make a truce.

Promise yourself happiness to find.

Accumulating sorrow will take you down,

Daily wearing the widow's gown!

Sabotaging your-self to comfort the hollow!

Just do what you love, and love will follow.

I did that and I paid my price.

I stood tall as I threw my dice.

Euphoria I needed but I couldn't afford!

So I took the road that does not bind.

I sat among vultures sipping my tea,

Wondering to see or not to see!

Turning a blind eye on my pride,

To learn the secrets of being kind!

I owned nothing and nothing owned me,

I was just wrestling with the so many me.

I challenged my fate against a chancy storm,

To reach my heaven—I had to reform.

Sometimes my madness made much sense,

Appraising my core at my vanity's expense!

Penury I tasted and I don't mind,

All my excess led me home.

Chapter 14

A Sinner Becomes a Saint!

While I thought I was walking with the vain cattle,

I was walking with God.

And while my child within, took god by the hand, to lead Him to my

vision's way,iHim

I was being led!

And while I thought it was noble to be honey to the bitter,

I was collecting sticky bugs.

And while I was thought that I can heal viciousness with kindness,

I was attracting disparaging thugs.

Meanwhile, I cultivated my nature,

Meditating daily on the divine order,

On a humble rug!

Thanking God now for the rose, along with its perfect thorns,

And knowing that somewhere in a dawn,

A miracle is born.

Open your heart, dear one, but only to the kind.

The scorpion friend, keep away and away is not behind!

He'll sting you no matter what; the twist is in his nature's mind.

His poison is fed by your tears, in misery, with him you'll wind.

A loving vibration do attract,

A noble destiny is on the call.

And once you know where you should go,

Life will show you that you're on track.

Selfish you're not, when you search your joy,

What can you give if you have it not?

In rage, we judge, pity, and endanger.

To us, compassion is an icy stranger.

Fenced with their envy, what to face?!

Glow with light or hide with lace?

Getting lost in darkness we impetuously roam,

Wondering, where's that inner ranger!

I'm fighting for happiness, brothers,

So I love and shine, and to the mystery I yield,

Even if light is to their darkness sour.

As I heal, I dare to see what's real,

And hope one day to the light I'll lead.

Heavenly Mother,

I surrender to this new birth in this new field,

In the kingdom of light lit with angel's fairies dust, forever, and every hour.

Where my addiction is to happiness—and maybe ours—

Where the adoration shrine is love, not fear, and blessed we feel!

To have the good, send and do the good, just what you could,

And in your every step, try to plant any kind of flower.

Yes, we have shown love and light with half a heart.

When injustice we caused, and maybe violence provoked—

And saw suffering and looked the other way!

When our pain was heavier than the will to play!

When we were buried and defeated by evil's worth,

When he was our companion, and with him we spoke!

And our ego was hungry and ready to devour;

And our prey we lavishly stroked.

We all were busy sometimes capturing the power.

Remorse we felt, and our souls were wrenched,

And forgiveness we asked on a holy bench

Scenting an angel in a candle breeze,

Hoping the sinner becomes a saint.

Saying forgive me, lord, for being cruel,

And for being a predator to hoard the fuel—

I need a storm for my spirit to scour!

But still thinking: Isn't that how life awoke?!

With a Bing and a Bang, and a predator cow, and a prey cower?

Where does violence stop and peace begin?

Will nature ever change its rules?

Can its laws be someday thrown?!

Is it our psyche or it ain't?!

Or shall I simply hide by an angel in a bower?

The question is and still remains—Of course!

But the answer is in your conscious which has grown.

Easy to steer a fool, and difficult to drive a mule,

Each its restraint!

Ideas can be twisted with a capital defence,

And can levy distraint.

Yes—most are harder when decorated by a throne.

And any crowd of stone is more appealing when on the Rhône,

Still a constraint!

But your heart knows the truth, that's innate.

 It's your source.

Armed with instinct and wisdom, your inner force,

And a God within, a modest, fair, and optimistic one—

Who believes still in his children, in you!

Your destiny you can still repaint.

Where no one needs to bully but with respect guide—

A world led by deferential exchange,

Where we carry those who might lead us to the holy ride

It's time for a rebirth. It's time for the change.

But first, remember daughter, and son!

Illumination favours the good and kind yet bold.

Here, you've been warned and told.

So if you hear that stillness sound,

Blessed you are, there's no dearth.

Know that abundance in all what's good,

To all who choose to heal their soul!

So if you grieve now, it's not in vain.

The sun will shine upon you, that's God's domain.

Start by saying in every wake,

Good morning God. Good morning life.

I want a rebirth— I want my soul to sublimate.

Now, here is a goal!

And enjoy your summer—and the Lord's mirth—

By accepting to be an angel on earth!

Chapter 15

Enchanted New Beginning

A prayer for the light and heaven's gateway:

Thank you, my lord, for this enchanted new beginning in a wonderful world,

filled with heavenly abundance, surprising miracles, magnificent creations,

sublime creatures, divine light, pure love, self-respect, happiness, joy,

noble energy of exchange, and brilliance.

Where I see things that I appreciate, enjoy, and praise.

Where I'm in a constant state of gratitude, grace, serenity, and inner peace,

as in the heart of wonder I gaze.

Where I'm in harmony with my truth and integrity whenever, and wherever

I may be.

Where my answered prayers reflect back on me with inspired ideas,

signs, along with a blessed smile.

Where God also lives in my heart, soul, and mind.

Where I radiate hope, because I know that you love, support,

and accept me for who I am, even when I'm to your cause sometimes blind.

Yet you still guide me to my evolution, my new stages of development and insight,

and help me with my inner fight.

Yes, thank you, my friends in heaven, for your love, protection, blessings,

and allowing me to have the courage, and honesty to see, and do what's right.

Only to divinity the road I choose. And by my heart's call I shall abide.

Knowing that love is not on my door, but in my inner fire's light resides.

I choose you, as you chose me, and that is my might!

Throughout my earthly journey, my lord,

Allow me please to constantly heal my soul, body, spirit, and mind.

That's what I am now after; that's what I want to find.

To have the strength to find meaning, and delight, in all what's possible—

To always know a greater form of life, filled with caring, sharing, loving, and giving.

And after I'm healed, let me others heal.

And with this generous spirit, miracles are real.

I know you are here, I know you are near.

I know you hear me, I know you guide me,

I know as we know our biggest grace of all, and the heart felt dear.

Thank you for this soaring flight.

I can now fly pondering above and beneath,

Yet there is no more fear to fall.

With this genuine faith, my life is prodigious and bright.

Help me, my lord, with my evolution,

Let me be each day better than yesterday,

That I will be part of the solution!

I know from my perfection I'm still far!

Shadows that block me are still here,

And I wish I knew what they are!

Help me release them so I can progress,

They make me weak, I must confess.

Give me freedom, give me light!

Manifest your favour day and night.

Serene and happy I must remain,

That's who I am, not the vain.

I dance in your noble forms,

Not only the human norms.

And for that indeed I am very grateful,

Living in your heart must be fateful.

While by your side, I still ask,

To repulse every evil and shatter their masks!

To be a magnet to all what's good.

To become the best I ever could.

Dear lord, I do pray,

To live in your divine grace,

With my open soul to the arms of life!

To freely receive your joyous blessings,

That hail upon me with heavenly pace.

To find and give the best of me,

And every mist becomes your face.

Knowing that you'll accompany me,

In my every move till I reach that place!

To always be grateful for the divine chance.

To love, be loved, to sing and dance.

To believe in the incredible now and ever

To reflect your divinity, nothing else, and else never

To be your light, the revealer of inner treasures

And have the courage to stay alone, and discover.

To be in your joy, whenever and forever

Imprint your smile in my soul, so I may be radiant, brilliant, sweet, and

clever.

To accept me to be among your angels, on earth and wherever

To instruct me through my dreams to the howsoever

Please, my lord, through my inner call,

Lead me to my happiness, spiritual growth, goodness, godliness, and your

laughter.

Where you beckon and guide me.

I believe in the incredible, I believe in you.

I believe in a good world, I believe in the divine,

Where among angels,

I will on my own marvelous world reign. *Amen*!

But first, in my stillness sound,

A sudden urge emerges from the no-where.

Gently, secretly, calling me to Spanish Sees!

My heart finds itself rejoicing, as again, welcomes the unknown.

27th of January 2007

What's that stillness?! What's that sound?

Is it silence?! That drives me to numbness,

With no ground? What's that game?!

Is it my mind? Going insane?

What's that question?! Who am I?!

That old refrain— In vain, in vain!

www.ingramcontent.com/pod-product-compliance
Lightning Source LLC
Chambersburg PA
CBHW020844260626
47169CB00003B/1135